Can You Say Catastrophe?

Saturday, April 20, 1:45 pm

my 13th birthday

(unfortunately)

Here's the good news: my instincts were right.

Here's the bad news: The party was so much worse than I could have

ever imagined. It was the most embarrassing day of my entire life.

It started when I woke up this morning, but it went from bad to ca-

tastrophic when Dad made Mary, _____, and me all make a wish and

blow out our candles. I wished for _____ now so the party would be

over. but the _____ didn't give with my _____ puff. I wondered to my-

self _____ wish wasn't coming true. It's too bad, because when _____

happened at her party, we birthday pie was the one of those

moments in a movie that's so crucial, you can't believe it even though you

thought it _____ because it would never happen in real life. Not in this

_____ at all.

I was talking to Emma and _____, and Mary _____ over. She asked if

to pick _____ up _____ Billy. He laughed and told mom it'd be

easier for so long, grabbed Billy by the legs and _____ him up

(pretty easily, actually) and held him in the air long enough to attract

the attention of her friends, who walked over to see _____

_____

"_____ are you _____ he picked up?" she asked _____

By the time _____ there was a lineup of ten _____ boys who wanted to be

caught, flung, and rocketed up _____. One by _____, my brother _____ every

_____ and tossed them in the air. There's always that one kid who is

_____ ty, much as _____.

THE MOSTLY MISERABLE LIFE
OF APRIL SINCLAIR

Can You Say Catastrophe?

LAURIE FRIEDMAN

MINNEAPOLIS

Darby Creek
A division of Lerner Publishing Group, Inc.
241 First Avenue North
Minneapolis, MN 55401 U.S.A.

Website address: www.lernerbooks.com

Main body text set in Janson Text LT Std 12/17.
Typeface provided by Linotype AG.

Library of Congress Cataloging-in-Publication Data

Friedman, Laurie B., 1964–
    Can you say catastrophe? / by Laurie Friedman.
        pages cm. — (The mostly miserable life of April Sinclair, #1)
    ISBN 978–1–4677–0925–5 (trade hard cover : alk. paper)
    ISBN 978–1–4677–1620–8 (eBook)
    [1. Family life—Fiction. 2. Dating (Social customs)—Fiction.] I. Title.
PZ7.F89773Cao 2013
    [Fic]—dc23   2012048867

Manufactured in the United States of America
1 – BP – 7/15/13

For my parents and my sisters.
My story began at home.

Home is where your story begins.

Saturday, April 20, 11:45 p.m.
My 13th birthday
(unfortunately)

Here's the good news: my instincts were right.

Here's the bad news: The party was so much worse than I could have ever imagined. It was the most embarrassing day of my entire life.

It started when I woke up this morning, but it went from bad to catastrophic when Dad made May, June, and me all make a wish and blow out our candles. I wished for a down-pour so the party would be over, but the sky stayed light blue with little puffy white clouds, and I knew my wish wasn't coming true. It's too bad, because what happened after every-one ate birthday pie was like one of those mo-ments in a movie that's so awful, you can't believe the filmmaker thought it up because it would never happen in real life. But in this case, it did.

I was talking to Billy and Brynn, and May walked over. "You want me to pick you up?" she asked Billy. He laughed and told May he'd love to see her try. So May grabbed Billy by the legs and lifted him up (pretty easily, actually) and held him in the air long enough to get the at-tention of her friends, who walked over to see what was going on.

"Who else wants to be picked up?" she asked.

Before I knew it, there was a lineup of ten-year-olds who wanted to see if May could pick them up. One by one, she picked up everyone in the line and held them in the air for a few seconds. Her friends were cheering. May was grinning.

"I bet you can't pick up somebody really big," one of her friends said.

May nodded her head like she accepted the dare, and then she looked around the backyard. Her eyes stopped on the tallest kid at the party—Matt Parker.

She started across the yard to where he was standing. I didn't like where this was going. "Don't!" I yelled. I tried to grab May and stop her, but before I could, she had her arms wrapped around Matt's legs. The next thing I knew, he was hovering five inches above the ground.

Matt looked like he couldn't believe some little kid was lifting him off the ground. I couldn't either. Everyone crowded around and watched as May held Matt up for what felt like forever. There was clapping and whistling. Matt looked like he was in shock.

"Who are you?" asked May when she finally put him down.

Matt regained his composure and smiled.

He has the whitest teeth and the cutest smile. My heart stopped.

"Matt Parker. I just moved in next door."

For a brief second, I thought maybe the worst was over, but that's when June decided to chime in. She looked right at Matt. "April said you're hot and that she doesn't even know you yet but she already has a crush on you."

I couldn't believe what I heard—what everyone over the age of six and under fourteen in Faraway, Alabama, heard too. I had to do some damage control. "What are you talking about?" I made a face like no one should believe a word that was coming out of June's mouth.

But June was nodding her head like she knew exactly what she was talking about. She pointed at me. "I heard you say those *exact* words to Brynn just a few minutes ago."

Everyone looked at Brynn. I tried to send a message to her brain to be a good best friend and tell everyone that my sister was a pathological liar. But unfortunately, that's not what Brynn did. She just stood there and grinned, like she thought the whole thing was funny.

Later, Brynn tried to explain that all she did was smile and that she didn't confirm that what June said was true. But here's the problem: she didn't say it wasn't true either!

Everyone was looking at me. I heard whispers and laughter. And just like that, I was stuck in the middle of the worst moment of my life. Matt raised his eyebrows at me, shook his head without saying anything, and then walked off. But his face said it all, and what it said was, *get me out of here!*

All I can say is, Matt Parker, take me with you! Take me somewhere far away. But wait! The joke's on me—I'm already in Faraway.

Sunday, April 21, 9:14 A.M.
In bed
Where I plan to stay
For a very long time

I don't know if it's because as a teenager, my brain is capable of more complex thought or if what I'm about to write is just blatantly obvious, but there are ten very clear reasons why my life is miserable.

1. My mom, Flora. She was put on this planet to embarrass me. To be fair, she wasn't too bad during my first decade. But ever since I "went preteen" (Mom's words, not mine), it's like she ate some bad fish and hasn't been the same since.

2. My dad, Rex. He was put here to embarrass me too. My dad used to write a relationship advice column in our local newspaper. Now he's opening a restaurant called The Love Doctor Diner, so he'll be serving up advice *and* food.

3. My little sister May, age nine, almost ten, a.k.a. "The Brawn." Yesterday was Exhibit A of why having the strongest kid in town as a little sister is not always a good thing.

4. My baby sister, June, soon to be seven, a.k.a. "The Brain." Her motto in life is "Listen. Remember. Repeat." Mom says I need to be careful when June is around. I say my parents need to buy a muzzle and use it.

5. My dog, Gilligan. All he likes to do is

run away from home. I don't blame him. I'd like to run away too.

6. My town. I live in Faraway, Alabama. Yes, pronounced "far away." Some girls have it so good. When they meet people, they get to say things like, "Hi, I'm Chloe from New York," or "I'm Jasmine from Los Angeles." But I have to say, "I'm April from Faraway." Imagine the looks you get with that one.

7. My nose. It's shaped like a ball of bread dough. Brynn told me I should be doing this exercise where you press two fingers against the sides of your nose for twenty minutes a day to give it shape. So far, no results.

8. My butt. It's tiny. A lot of girls at school have nice round butts—Billy says they're bootylicious. I plan on asking God for some help in the bootylicious department, but I want him to get to the boob thing first. (See below.)

9. My boobs. They're uneven. One is an A. The other is a B. THIS CAN'T BE

NORMAL! I need to Google this to see what can be done.

10. My mouth. Quite often it says the wrong thing. Especially when it is talking to cute boys.

Ten more reasons . . .

Ha! Just kidding. I could go on like this all day.

I really could.

3:42 P.M.
Still stuck on yesterday

I don't want to think about my birthday party, but it's all my brain will let me think about. And what I keep thinking is that I should have known it was going to be a disaster. There were so many signs, from the moment I opened my eyes, and I ignored them all.

I should have known when May and June woke me up wearing matching floral patchwork pants and T-shirts that Mom had obviously made and sneakers with sunflowers glued on them, and Mom handed me a third matching outfit.

I should have known when June started rambling about a birthday party for the three of us with a "Spring Has Sprung" theme, and a sign that Mom hung in the backyard that said "Celebrate Our Spring Flowers, April, May, and June," and a Pin the Stem on the Rose game that Dad set up.

I should have known when I reminded Mom that I wanted to have a skating party and she said, "April, everyone has skating parties. Dare to be different. Your father and I have put a lot of time and thought into all of your birthdays this year. Today will be unique!"

I should have known when Billy and Brynn showed up—my best friends, the ones who are supposed to love me more than anyone (except maybe my family who doesn't really count)—and couldn't stop laughing at what I was wearing.

I should have known when I saw that the party was catered by Dad's new restaurant. Dad stuck signs in all the food saying "From the

Love Doctor Diner—Grand opening Friday, May 3!" It was like half party, half promotional event.

And I definitely should have known it was going to be a disaster when Matt Parker, world's hottest new boy next door, showed up and introduced himself, to which I replied "Welcome to the neighborhood!" like an old lady. And then, of course, I told Brynn—apparently too loudly—"He's so hot. I don't even know him, and I already have a crush on him."

The rest is history.

I read this quote once that said, "The past is history. The future is a mystery. All we have is the present." That might be true, but what I know at present is that I should have seen the signs and spent my thirteenth birthday in bed. I'm not blaming myself entirely, though. I blame my parents. I wasn't part of the planning that went into having three daughters born in the spring and naming them all after their birth months, and I certainly didn't ask to have a party with my sisters where we all wore matching outfits.

I hate my birthday. I know that sounds dramatic, but it's true. I've been scarred for life. And I'm only thirteen.

It's the friends you can

call up at 4 A.M. that matter.

—*Marlene Dietrich*

Thursday, April 25, 5:35 P.M.
Just home from Billy's house
Super fun but super weird afternoon

This afternoon at Billy's started out really fun, but then something happened that I wasn't expecting, and super fun turned to super weird.

Fun part first. Billy and Brynn and I went to Billy's after school to finish our Science Fair project. (That wasn't the fun part.) After we put everything on our display board and wrote our conclusion, we were sitting on the floor of Billy's family room drinking lemonade and eating popcorn and mini Reese's—our snacks of choice since third grade when the three of us vowed to always be best friends and eat the same after-school snack for the rest of our lives, or at least our school lives. That's when the fun part happened.

Billy and Brynn and I were sitting on the floor with Billy's mom's iPad, looking at old photos of Billy, Brynn, and me from grade school. There were pictures of us from birthday parties, school plays, and holidays. "Aww, we were so cute!" I said, pointing to a picture from fifth grade of us all dressed like hippies on Halloween.

When Billy pulled up a picture of the three of us from Colonial Night in third grade, we all collapsed into a laughing heap. Billy was George Washington, I was Martha Washington, and Brynn was Betsy Ross. We looked so funny in our costumes. That was the night we became friends, when Brynn and I couldn't stop laughing at Billy's jokes about wig troubles, and we've been inseparable ever since. The Three Musketeers—that's what Billy's dad calls us.

Honestly, I don't know what I'd do without my friends. Even though Brynn can have her moments, she's been my best friend since kindergarten. She's an only child, so she's more like a sister I actually like than a friend. And Billy has kept me laughing since the day I met him.

Like today, when he did his recap of what happened to Charlie Bonner in fifth-period math. I saw it when it happened, but it was even funnier when Billy put his spin on it. First of all, no one likes Charlie because he always makes fun of other people. But today he got back everything he's ever dished out.

Charlie hates our math teacher, Ms. Crawford, and, to be fair, with good reason. Ms. Crawford always calls on Charlie to come to the board to work out the problems no one else can figure out. So today, when she called on Charlie, he was prepared to get back at her. He had an egg in his shorts pocket and he told everyone before class he was going to crack it on Ms. Crawford's head when she called him up to the board. I have to admit, I couldn't wait to see him do it, but what happened was so much funnier. The egg broke in Charlie's pocket when he was walking up to the board. There must have been a hole in his pocket, because egg was dripping down his leg as he stood in front of the class.

"The yellow part looked like petrified pee, and I won't say what the white part looked like," said Billy to Brynn and me.

Billy was pretending to do the problem on the board and shifting around and covering up his pants with his hands. It was a spot-on imitation of what Charlie looked like this afternoon. I laughed so hard, lemonade came out of my nose. Brynn had to run to the bathroom.

When we finally stopped laughing, Brynn brought up one of our favorite topics: camp.

"Fifty-one days till we leave!" she said.

Every year, Brynn does the countdown to Camp Silver Shores, and she's always the one who makes sure we have everything on the list neatly packed in our duffels.

"I can't wait to go," I told Billy and Brynn. "Four amazing weeks with no parents or sisters to drive me crazy. My mom is making me nuts. My birthday party was a nightmare."

Brynn nodded like she agreed. "Total nightmare."

I cringed. It was one of those times when you don't actually want anyone to agree with you. I love Brynn like a sister, but I don't always like when she says whatever's on her mind. Lately, she's into this whole I-want-to-be-a-journalist-when-I-grow-up thing, and she says good journalists aren't afraid to speak the truth. Which is fine if the person talking is on TV, and they don't know you, but not always fine if they're your best friend.

Anyway, when Brynn said my party was a total nightmare, I ran my tongue over my teeth, which Billy says I do when I'm nervous. Billy looked at me and caught me doing it, and that's when the thing happened that made the afternoon SUPER WEIRD.

Billy smiled at me in a sweet way. "I thought you looked cute at your party," he said, like he really did think I looked cute. Then, he stretched his leg across the carpet and touched my big toe with his. Our toes just kind of sat there for a minute, touching each other like they had minds of their own and they didn't want to stop touching.

IT WAS SO WEIRD!

Our body parts have touched before, but somehow this time it felt different, like Billy was touching me on purpose. I looked at Brynn to see if she noticed, but she didn't look like she thought anything seemed weird or different. She just kept going on about camp.

Even if Brynn couldn't feel the difference, I could.

I looked at Billy to see if he could feel the difference too, but he wasn't looking at me. He was looking at his mom's iPad like he was trying hard to find one particular photo. Then, he curled his toe away from mine like he wasn't even sure he knew it had been there in the first place.

Billy was acting like nothing was any different. So I acted like nothing was any different. But to be honest, things felt a little different.

Complete humiliation

Can you go to jail for locking your younger sisters in the attic until you're old enough to leave for college? I don't care. I'm taking my chances. I hate them. They have zero respect for my privacy.

Tonight, after I showered, I came into my room and locked the door. I read in a magazine that if you stand with your back arched, it makes your butt look bigger. I really want my butt to look bigger, so I dropped my towel, looked in the mirror, arched my back and stuck my butt out. It actually did look bigger. I touched it to see if it felt bigger, but it felt the same.

Then I looked in the mirror at my front.

The article I read also said scientific evidence suggests that stimulation of breasts makes them grow faster. The only boob I really want to grow is my left one. So while I was standing there naked with my back arched, I rubbed my left boob. I waited to see if anything happened, but it didn't, so I rubbed it a little harder. The article didn't give specifics on how long to do it, so I kept rubbing.

But then the worst thing happened.

I heard giggling, and it was coming from under my bed. I snatched up my bedspread, and my evil, spying little sisters were not only hiding under my bed, they had my cell phone! May started snapping pictures of me. Naked! I grabbed my phone and both of their arms and pulled them out from under the bed. May was laughing like crazy, and June was rubbing her chest and imitating me.

I've never screamed so loud in my life. "GET OUT! YOU'RE NEVER ALLOWED BACK IN HERE! IF YOU EVER SO MUCH AS TOUCH MY PHONE AGAIN, YOU'RE DEAD!"

I pushed them out the door and slammed it shut behind them. After I deleted the naked pictures of myself on my own phone, I kept screaming at them through the closed door. But all I heard was more laughing. I'm so furious. My throat hurts from screaming.

And I still have one boob that's smaller than the other.

10:52 P.M.

I can't sleep. I can't stop thinking about everything that happened today. Billy's toe touching mine. Naked pictures of me on my own phone. A boob that refuses to grow. Fifty-one days till camp. I can't wait to go away with my best friends and leave my sisters and parents behind for four perfect weeks. Mom just came into my room to tell me it's time to turn my light off. Which part of her doesn't understand that I'm thirteen?

She doesn't need to come into my room to tell me to turn my light off. What is the point of being a teenager if you can't make simple decisions like when to turn off your light?

Friday, April 26, 5:45 P.M.
The humiliation continues

I was just forced to roam the streets of my neighborhood yelling for my dog. Sadly, for me, it was not the first time this has happened.

Even more sadly, I know it will not be the last.

There is no love sincerer

than the love of food.

—*George Bernard Shaw*

Friday, May 3, 4:45 P.M.
I'm a torture victim

Tonight is the grand opening of the Love Doctor Diner. The night when everyone in Faraway is going to be at the diner. The night that my mom has made matching red vinyl jackets for my entire family with the logo of the Love Doctor Diner embroidered across the back of them. She's insisting we all wear jeans and white Ts and the jackets she made. This is cruel and unusual punishment for being born into what is clearly the wrong family for me. I'm not even sure it is my family. It seems so obvious that in no way do I share DNA with these people.

I don't want any part of this. I'm going into the kitchen to speak my mind.

4:53 p.m.

I'm back from the kitchen. I spoke my mind and, as usual, no one (specifically Mom) cared what I had to say.

"I'm not wearing this," I said to Mom and handed her back the jacket she made.

"You're not wearing this?" She repeated what I said, but she didn't say it like a statement. She said it like a question that was so absurd it didn't need to be answered. Then she handed me back the jacket and told me to go get ready, because we had an opening to go to and Dad was counting on all of us to do our parts.

I didn't like the sound of that. "What does 'do our parts' mean?" I asked.

Mom made her you're-going-to-like-this face, and instinctively, I knew I wasn't. "We're all going to be servers tonight." She said it like it was going to be a grand adventure that my entire family was taking together. Maybe May and June and Mom and Dad are taking it, but there's not a chance I'm going to serve pie to my friends in a tricked-out jacket.

"NO WAY!" I yelled at Mom. Then I kept on going, even though I knew by the look on her face that I should stop. "I'm thirteen now, and you can't keep telling me what to do."

It wasn't the first time I'd had this kind of talk with Mom. Just this morning before school, I was at the kitchen table trying to finish my math homework, and Mom kept standing over me asking why I hadn't finished my homework last night. I could hardly think to do my math, so I stopped trying to divide fractions and looked up at her.

Me: Do you know what a helicopter parent is?
Mom: Do YOU know what a helicopter parent is?
Me: I asked you first.
Mom: Don't get fresh with me, young lady.

The conversation with her completely ruined a perfectly good plate of frozen waffles.

So this afternoon, I crossed my arms and waited for the full effect of my words to sink in. I waited for Mom to say something reasonable like, "I'm sorry, April. Of course, you're a teen-ager now and you deserve to make your own decisions." But all she said was, "Young lady, this is not a democracy. Now go get dressed. Tonight is an important night for your father, and we're leaving soon."

Blah. Blah. Blah. Blah. Blah. On a scale of 1 to 10, I think tonight is going to be a -44.

10:35 P.M.

I was wrong about tonight. It was a -3,456,789.

It was the most embarrassing night ever. When Mom, May, June, and I got to the diner, Dad was already setting up. There were tables of food, racks of pies, and strolling musicians. The whole place, which is already heavy on the hearts motif, was decorated with extra hearts. There were hearts hanging on the walls and stuck to the windows and printed on the nap-kins. Dad even had heart-shaped candles and heart glitter confetti he gave to May and June and me to sprinkle across the tables. The whole thing looked like something Brynn and I would have made up to play when we were seven. The only kind-of cool thing Dad had was a blackboard by the front door with the pie and quote of the day written on it, kind of like they do at Starbucks. I love finding cool quotes, and the quote he had written on the blackboard tonight was one that I found and gave him.

Anyway, when we were done sprinkling confetti, Dad lined us up and gave us what he called our "marching orders." Serve pie. Be friendly. Make sure people enjoy themselves. More blah, blah, blah about how we are the Ambassadors of Love at the Love Doctor Diner, and it's up to us to make people want to come back and eat here again.

The Ambassadors of Love? What planet is my dad from?

Before I could beg him to shutter up before he opened, people started pouring in. Everyone I have ever known was there. My grandmother, my aunts, my cousins, my friends, my teachers, my neighbors, my pediatrician, our vet, the lady who works at the dry cleaners, the man who runs the concession stand at the baseball park, the lifeguard from the pool, even the crossing guard from my school.

"Go!" said Dad, like it was time to spring into action.

He handed May and June plates of what he says will be his world-famous pecan pie. He tried to give me one. "Take this pie to Mrs. Wallace," he said.

I didn't budge. I rolled my eyes in the direction of my overweight neighbor. "I don't think Mrs. Wallace needs pie." But Dad seemed to disagree. He took my arm and gave me an I-don't-like-your-attitude look. "Young lady, I expect you to be pleasant around the customers." Then he stuck the plate in my hand and sent me off.

There were lots of things I wanted to say to Dad, like: Do I look like I'm wearing a T-shirt that says waitress on it? Did I ask you to open a restaurant with a neon sign of a heart with a stethoscope wrapped around it right in the middle of town? And if the answer to all these questions is no, why am I stuck serving pie? But I couldn't ask any of those questions. All I could do was pull my jacket up around my ears and hand out pie to everyone I know. It was bad enough handing it to old ladies from my neighborhood, but it was complete humiliation handing it to my friends.

Brynn and her parents got there first. "April, I've always loved you in red," said Mrs. Stephens. She wrapped a bangle-braceleted arm around me and smiled as if she actually liked what I was wearing. Brynn's mom is very fashionable and she's always nice, but unlike her daughter, she's not always brutally honest. I know she wouldn't have been caught dead in a jacket like mine.

Brynn's dad was nice too. When he saw me, he wrapped his big arm around me and asked how his "other daughter" was doing.

Brynn wasn't as nice as her parents. I don't think she was trying to be not-nice—she was just being Brynn. When I handed her a plate of pie, she stuck her pretend journalist mic in my face. "Tell us, April Sinclair, do you think red vinyl will be in this fall?"

When Billy and his family arrived, things went from bad to worse.

Billy and I have barely spoken since the toe-touching incident, which is totally weird because we usually talk every day, but he hardly said anything to me in school all week. It's not like we're mad at each other. It's just like we're pretending the other person doesn't exist. I wouldn't be pretending that, except Billy is, so I'm stuck doing it back and I'm not even sure why.

It's confusing, and to make matters worse, I can't talk to Brynn about it. I know if I tell her about Billy's toe touching mine and that I think it happened in more-than-just-an-accident way, she'll say I'm crazy. She'll say that the three of us are best friends and that toes or other body parts touch all the time, especially when we're doing things like lying around on the floor. Then, she'll probably say something that she'll consider to be totally honest like, "April, do you think you're being a good friend when you make it seem like Billy likes you more than he likes me?"

That's what I was thinking when Billy and his family walked into the diner.

"There are the Weisses," said Dad. He handed me plates and pushed me in their direction. "Please help them find a place to sit."

I wanted someone else to give them pie and help them find a table, but they were already looking at me and it was pretty clear that's what I was supposed to do. I steered them through the crowds of people laughing and talking and eating every known Southern delicacy.

When I gave them their pie, Dr. and Mrs. Weiss both said they could use some pie after the drive over.

"Ha, ha," said Bobby, Billy's older brother, who got his license last week. "My driving isn't that bad."

Dr. Weiss laughed like he was just teasing Bobby.

All the Weisses were chatty except for Billy. It was so un-Billy-like. I guess it's what Billy has been like lately. Normally, he would say something to make me laugh, but tonight, he just sat there eating his pie.

I didn't really want to stand there and not talk to Billy, so I walked off like I had some official Love Doctor Diner server business to take care of. That was a big mistake because the person I walked into was Matt Parker. I actually walked right into him.

He stepped back and looked at me. "Cool top," he said.

"It's a jacket," I said back. The minute the words left my mouth, I regretted them. What's wrong with me? Why would I say something so dumb?

Matt shrugged like he didn't care if it was a top or a jacket.

I could feel my face turning as red as my jacket. I tried to think of something clever to say, but while I was thinking, Matt just said, "See ya," and walked off.

He must think I'm a total freak.

I certainly looked like one.

Saturday morning, May 4
Too early to even write the exact time

All I wanted to do this morning was sleep

off the humiliation of having to serve pie in a custom-made jacket to my not-so-secret crush. However, sleeping is now impossible because apparently Gilligan chose to leave home early and my Dad went out looking for him.

The sun isn't even up, but I am. Listening to my Dad yelling for my dog outside my window. My only hope is that this is all a nightmare, and that I'll go back to sleep, wake up, and see that my family is normal, my dog is asleep by my bed, and that I'm one of those girls who always says cute, clever things to boys.

Still Saturday morning
A little later
Still too early to write the exact time

I couldn't fall back asleep, which means two things:

1. What I hoped was just a terrible dream was not.

2. I'm going to the kitchen to eat pancakes.

9:17 A.M.
Back in my room

I went to the kitchen. One of the good things about my mom is that she always makes pancakes on Saturday mornings. Except, guess what was for breakfast this Saturday morning? Leftover pie.

Who feeds pie to their children for breakfast?

I officially hate pie.

A kiss is a lovely trick designed by nature to stop speech when words become superfluous.

—Ingrid Bergman

Wednesday, May 8, 8:45 p.m.
In my room with the door locked

OMG! The most unbelievable thing happened today. I'm not even really sure it happened, except that I know it did.

It started this morning after homeroom when I told Brynn I wanted to download some new music to my phone, and Billy asked if I wanted him to come over after school and help. Billy knows more about music than anybody I know, plus it was the first time he's spoken to me since the toe-touching thing, so I was like,

"Yeah, I'd love that."

When Billy came over, he didn't say a word about why he hasn't said a word to me in a week. We just started talking and laughing and listening to music like we always do.

Anyway, we were listening to music in my room, but it was hard to do because May and June were outside my door singing. They wouldn't stop and they were really annoying. "We're trying to set a world record for singing the longest without stopping," said May.

"We're trying to set a world record for singing the longest without stopping," repeated June.

"GO AWAY! FAR AWAY!" I yelled over the noise. They were driving me crazy. They just kept singing, and June kept repeating everything May was saying and they were really loud.

I put my fingers in my ears like I couldn't take another second, but Billy pulled them out. "Want me to get them to stop?" he asked.

I laughed at Billy. He's good at a lot of things, but I knew even he couldn't reason with the real-life versions of Thing One and Thing

Two. "No way can you get them to stop," I said.

That's when Billy made his I'm-always-up-for-a-challenge face. "Watch me."

He opened my door. "You two have awesome voices," he said to May and June. He sounded so sincere, like he was listening to Katy Perry singing in person and was blown away.

Just like that, May and June were quiet. Billy kept talking, slowly, like he was thinking about their talent and trying to decide what to do with it. "You have a very distinct sound. I think you could make an album."

Now May and June were really quiet. They were hanging on every word Billy was saying. He crossed his arms and rubbed his chin. "I've got it," he said. "Why don't you write your own songs?" He went and got a stack of paper and pens off my desk and handed it to them. "Really put some thought into what you want to sing, and then write your songs. You should write a lot of them. You're really good. When you're done, you need to practice singing each one." Then he went and got Dad's old tape recorder out of the top of my closet. Honestly, I don't even think it works, but they didn't know that. He handed it to them. "When you're done practicing, record your songs on this. Then we'll see if we can find someone to turn them into a real album."

May started jumping up and down. "Are we going to be famous?" she asked Billy.

"Are we going to be famous?" repeated June.

Billy nodded his head slightly like he thought it was a definite possibility.

"We're going to be famous!" they were both screaming and jumping. Before I knew it, May and June took the paper and the pens and the tape recorder, and they were gone. As loud as it had been in my room only moments before, suddenly it was completely quiet.

"You're amazing," I said. I did this little bow like I was worshipping Billy. But when I came back up, something happened that was even more amazing than Billy getting my sisters to go away.

Billy caught my hands like it was possible I might fall over and he wanted to make sure I didn't. I gave him a look like I wasn't going to fall over, but he didn't let go of my hands. Then he leaned over and kissed me.

ON THE LIPS!

He kissed me just for a few seconds and in a light, soft way, like I was a fragile doll that might break if he pressed too hard, but he definitely kissed me. It wasn't like the toe-touching where I wasn't sure if he knew our toes had touched or not. Our lips definitely touched, and we both knew they did.

I didn't move. I wasn't sure what to do. Then, almost as soon as Billy started kissing me, he stopped, and looked at me. "I've wanted to do that for a long time," was all he said.

I looked at Billy. I wasn't sure what to say. I was confused. First, the toe-touching. I thought I felt something, but it seemed like Billy didn't, so I pretended I didn't. Then he practically stopped talking to me, and then he said he wanted to come over and help me download music. It seemed like everything was back to normal, and then he kissed me. Part of me wanted to ask him why he kissed me and part of me just wanted him to kiss me again. All my thoughts were swirled together in my brain.

Billy and I stood there for a few seconds, looking at each other. Then, the next thing I knew, May and June barged into my room and our moment ended. Billy cleared his throat. "Is your album done?" he asked them.

"Not yet," said May. "Your mom called and said you have to go home for dinner. Now!"

"Now!" repeated June.

They had their hands on their hips like they were the dinner police, and it appeared they weren't going anywhere until Billy left. So he gave me a smile and walked out, but it was kind of a lopsided smile like he wasn't sure about what just happened.

And the truth is that I'm not sure about it either. It was my first kiss and it was with Billy. It sounds weird even saying it, but it was weird in a good way.

This morning, the only thing my brain was thinking about was what songs I was going to download on my phone. Now, my brain is thinking about so many different things.

What's it going to be like between Billy and

me now that we've kissed? Are we still friends? Are we more than friends? What's going to happen when we go to camp?

Should I tell Brynn what happened? I can't NOT tell Brynn what happened. I tell Brynn everything. And if Billy and I become more than just friends, Brynn will know anyway. But what's Brynn going to say? She always gets excited about stuff she calls "newsworthy," but I'm not sure she's going to be excited about this.

The thing is . . . Billy and Brynn and I have always been the Three Musketeers. Will we still be the Three Musketeers, or now will we be the Two Musketeers and a Hershey bar?

I'm not sure. Right now, the only thing I'm sure about is that there are lots of things I'm not sure about.

As we drive along this
road called life, occasionally a gal
finds herself a little lost.

—*Carrie Bradshaw*

Thursday, May 9, 7:45 A.M.
Homeroom

If I had naturally shiny, bouncy hair, this morning would have turned out differently. I set my alarm for 6:30 so I could get up and curl my hair. I needed a good hair day because I didn't want to see Billy for the first time after he kissed me and have him think he can't believe he kissed a girl with hair like mine.

I'm also planning to tell Brynn what happened with Billy.

I'm nervous to tell her because I'm not sure

how she's going to take it, but Brynn is the person I always talk to when something happens in my life that's worth talking about. It might sound silly, but I want to be having a good hair day when I tell one of my best friends about kissing my other best friend.

Anyway, when I went into the bathroom this morning, I couldn't find my curling iron, so I went into May's room. Even though she never uses the curling iron, she thinks hiding things I use is hilarious. "May, have you seen my curling iron?" I tried to ask in a sweet voice. Sometimes when I talk nicely, she'll just give me back my stuff.

But not today.

"It must be hiding," May said, like the curling iron was able to hide on its own.

"It must be hiding," said June, the backup choir.

I knew what was next. May was going to make me play hot or cold if I wanted to find my curling iron. I really wanted it, so I played. I looked under her bed and behind her dresser and inside her pillowcase. She kept saying hot and cold but not in a way that made any sense.

I kept looking at the clock. It was getting later and later, and my hair wasn't getting any curlier and it didn't seem like I was getting any hotter, so I did the only thing I could think of to speed up the process.

I grabbed May's hair and yelled, "GIVE ME MY CURLING IRON YOU LITTLE BRAT OR YOU'RE NOT GOING TO LIKE WHAT HAPPENS NEXT!"

Unfortunately for me, Mom walked by right then, and even though all I'd done was try to get back what belongs to me, I was the one who got in trouble.

"April Elizabeth Sinclair, what are you doing? That is unacceptable behavior." Then Mom went on for a long time about how as the oldest sister, it's my responsibility to treat my younger sisters in a manner that teaches them how to treat other people. Homeroom is way too short to write about all the blah, blah, blah. The only thing I have to say is that my hair looks like crap because Mom went on for so long, I didn't get my curling iron back in time to use it.

10:47 A.M., Study Hall

OK. Not having curly hair is the least of my problems.

My biggest problem is Billy, who I've walked past three times since I got to school, and all three times he's ignored me. It's the same thing that happened after the toe-touching, but this time, after the kissing, it's worse. He's not talking to me OR looking at me. I don't get it.

Maybe no curls is my problem. I bet if I had curls, he'd be talking to me. Now I really have to talk to Brynn. I just looked over at Brynn, three desks away, and mouthed, "I have something HUGE to tell you at lunch." She nodded like she gets it.

I don't even care that it's fish stick day in the cafeteria. I can't wait for lunch to get here.

12:55 P.M., Girls' bathroom

Lunch didn't go as planned.

I thought Brynn would get that it would be for her ears only when I told her I had something HUGE to tell her. But today Brynn's mindreading skills were at an all-time low.

"Start talking!" she said as she dragged Billy over to the table where I was already sitting. It was so obvious to me Billy didn't want to be there, but it clearly was NOT obvious to Brynn.

"So . . . what's the HUGE thing that happened to you?" Brynn pretended to stick a microphone in front of my mouth. She poked Billy in the ribs. "Breaking news! April Sinclair has something to say. One. Two. Three. And April, you're on . . ." She pointed at me like cameras were rolling.

I couldn't move. Billy looked like he was going to throw up. Brynn leaned forward like she was enjoying the suspense. I tried to give Brynn a we'll-talk-later look. Billy gave me a keep-your-mouth-shut look. For three people who always have lots to say to each other, we were strangely silent.

It was complete awkwardness.

I had no idea what to do, so I did the only thing I could think of. I shoved a fish stick in my mouth, pretended to choke, and ran to the bathroom, which is where I am now and where I'm going to stay until lunch is over. Or possibly for the rest of my life, because on the way to the bathroom, I passed Matt Parker walking down the hall with a bunch of other eighth graders. He actually waved and said hi to me. Of course, I couldn't say anything back because my mouth was full of fish sticks.

5:15 P.M.

In my room

The rest of the school day was a disaster.

Brynn kept asking what it was I was going to tell her.

Billy kept glaring at me like I better not say anything.

There was nothing I could do that would make both friends happy. My head was a mess.

When Ms. Crawford called on me in math, I didn't even know what page we were on. How could I think about linear equations when my brain was thinking about how Billy was going to feel if I tell Brynn he kissed me and how Brynn is going to feel when I tell her? Brynn can be unpredictable. She's truth-in-journalism honest when she's the one asking the questions, but sometimes when I tell her stuff, she gets quiet like she's thinking something but doesn't want to say it. Part of me wishes I'd never told her I had something to tell her. But I can't un-tell it, so I asked Brynn if she wanted to go for ice cream after school and talk. We do our best talking over hot fudge sundaes.

But today wasn't one of our best talks. As soon as we got our ice cream and sat down, Brynn told me to start talking. So I just came right out and said it. "Billy kissed me."

Telling Brynn made it feel more real than it had before, even when it happened. I waited for her to say something. I wanted her to make one of her newsflash comments like, "Cute couple alert! April Sinclair and Billy Weiss hook up! This is a happy day in Faraway!"

I hoped she would stick her pretend mic in my mouth and ask for all the juicy details, or even get mad about it. But Brynn didn't do any of that.

There were a few "wows" and "tell me mores," but mostly, she was quiet while I told her exactly what happened in my room with

Billy. When I finished, she looked at me and nodded like she heard what I said. Then she ate her ice cream and didn't say much else. This was definitely one of those times when Brynn was thinking something she didn't want to say. I just wish I knew what that something was.

Friday, May 10, 7:53 A.M.
Homeroom
Good news and bad news

Good news first: I know what Brynn is thinking.

This morning, when I got to my locker, she had left me a note that said, "NEWSFLASH: April Elizabeth Sinclair gets her first kiss by 7th grade cutie Billy Weiss!" She drew hearts, lips, smiley faces, and X's and O's all over it. She signed it, LYLAS. Luv ya like a sister, Brynn.

I know the note was Brynn's way of saying she's cool with what happened.

She gave me a big hug after I read the note. Brynn really is the sister I wish I had.

Now the bad news: Billy saw Brynn hug me after I read the note. I know the look he gave me, and it was his way of saying he knows that the note and the hugging meant I told Brynn that he kissed me.

I also know the look was his way of saying he's not cool with the fact that I told Brynn. I've known Billy since third grade, and I've never seen him look mad.

Until today.

For it was not into my ear you whispered, but into my heart. It was not my lips you kissed, but my soul.

—Judy Garland

Saturday, May 11
11:30 A.M.

Billy has not spoken to me since Wednesday.

Sunday, May 12
5:43 P.M.

Billy has still not spoken to me. No calls. No texts. Nothing.

I went over to Brynn's house this afternoon to ask her what she thinks about Billy not talking to me just because he kissed me and he knows I told her. Brynn says I had to tell her because

I'm her best friend. Then she said that Billy is just "processing" and all he needs is a little time.

I asked her how much time she thinks he needs. Brynn said she thinks he'll talk to me at school tomorrow. She said that all the three of us ever do in school is talk, and if Billy doesn't talk, the only thing left to do will be his schoolwork. I reminded Brynn that Billy likes doing schoolwork. She said I had a point.

I guess we'll see what tomorrow brings.

Monday, May 13
7:47 P.M.

Tomorrow, which is now today, brought nothing. The only thing Billy did at school was a lot of schoolwork.

Tuesday, May 14
8:56 P.M.

Today Billy did even more schoolwork.

8:58 P.M.

Billy didn't talk to me today, but Matt Parker did. I was walking by the baseball field on the way back from P.E., and Matt said hi. For once, I wasn't a total blubbering idiot around him. I just smiled (in a pretty cute way, I think) and said hi back.

Ugh! I can't believe I just wrote that. It's pathetic that I'm proud of myself for just saying hi, but it was kind of an accomplishment given the fact that every other time Matt Parker has even looked in my direction, I've said something stupid. I don't even know why I'm writing this. I'm sure Matt saying hi meant nothing.

Absolutely nothing.

Wednesday, May 15
4:45 P.M.

I made a decision. If Billy's not going to talk to me, I'm going to talk to Billy. The only problem is that I'm not sure what to say to him, because I'm not even sure why he's not talking to me. It could be that he's mad because I told Brynn he kissed me. But I don't think that's the problem, because he wasn't talking to me before he thought I'd told Brynn. Or it could be he doesn't know what to say to me. That's what

Brynn thinks it is. She said she read in *Seventeen* that it's normal not to know what to say to people after you kiss them. But Billy always knows what to say. It could be that he's upset he kissed me in the first place. Maybe kissing me was one of those things that falls into the things-you-do-without-thinking-first category. Except that when he kissed me, he said he'd wanted to do it for a long time.

I'm confused. I'm going to brush my hair, put on lip gloss, and hope I get un-confused.

4:59 p.m.

I'm still confused, but at least I have smooth hair, shiny lips, and a plan.

I'm going to walk Gilligan over to Billy's house. I'm going to say I was just out walking my dog and happened to pass his house. But while I'm pretending to walk my dog past his house, I'm going to talk to Billy and find out exactly what's going on.

10:47 P.M.

In my room

My door is locked

My brain is spinning

What I'm about to write is CRAZY!

I never found out what's going on with Billy. I took Gilligan out for a walk like I'd planned, but then something completely un-planned happened.

I saw Matt Parker. He was walking his dog too and he was like, "Want to walk our dogs together?" He didn't even wait for an answer. He just started walking beside me and telling me all this stuff about how the best thing about living in Faraway is that they have a really good baseball team and that it's a lot better than the team he was on when he lived in California, and how he misses living near the Pacific Ocean be-cause he liked surfing there, and that he used to take all these cool pictures of the beach there, which he said looks totally different from the beaches here.

One minute, it seemed like Matt Parker hardly knew I was alive, and the next minute, he was telling me all this stuff about himself.

I wanted to say the right thing back, so I tried to think hard and fast. "The beaches around here are pretty cool," I said. I thought that still sounded kind of stupid, so I kept talking. "But I've never been to California. I bet the beaches there are awesome."

Matt smiled. "Want to see some pictures?" he asked.

And the next thing I knew, I was in Matt Parker's family room looking at the pictures he took of the beaches in California. I couldn't even believe it was me, sitting on a couch next to him, looking at pictures on his laptop. We looked for a long time, and then the most unbelievable thing happened.

Matt put his hand on my leg. At first, I thought maybe it was a mistake. But then he didn't move it. He looked at me in this way that's hard to describe, because no one's ever looked at me like that before. This sounds really weird, but it felt like he was trying to look inside me. I wanted to look away, but I couldn't. It was like Matt Parker's brain was talking to mine and telling it I should keep looking at him while he looked at me.

I'm not sure exactly what happened next. I remember thinking the room felt too warm. I wondered where Matt's parents were, but the house was quiet. It was just the two of us. After that, everything became a blur.

Matt put his laptop down. He squeezed my leg. Then he kissed me.

It wasn't anything like the way Billy kissed me. It wasn't soft, like I was a fragile doll. Matt Parker's lips were pressed against mine, and it was so intense. Part of me felt like I shouldn't be kissing anyone like that, but part of me liked it.

Matt put his hands on my waist. My cell phone vibrated in my back pocket. "Ignore it," mumbled Matt. He kissed me again. I tried to focus on kissing Matt, but my phone vibrated again and it was hard to ignore the buzzing of my phone against my butt.

In the corner of my brain, I heard Gilligan bark. Matt's lips were still locked against mine. His hands were tight around my waist. I felt the vibration of my phone again.

I pulled away and reached into my back pocket. I freaked. Mom had called three times.

I looked at the time. "My mom is going to kill me!" I told Matt. "I was supposed to be home an hour ago to go to my grandma's birthday dinner."

Matt did this head bob like I'd better go.

I grabbed Gilligan and raced home. And just like that, my unbelievable moment with Matt Parker ended, and my nightmare with my parents began.

The minute I walked into the kitchen, Mom said, "April, where have you been?"

My whole family was sitting there, dressed and ready to go.

Fortunately, Mom didn't wait for an answer to her question. She crossed her arms. She didn't look happy. "April, I told you to be back by 6:00 to go to Gaga's birthday dinner. What do you have to say for yourself?"

I tried to pull myself together. I prayed I didn't look like I'd been kissing my next-door neighbor. "I told you I was going to walk Gilligan," I reminded Mom. "I just forgot about the time." Which is true, I did forget about the time.

But that didn't seem to be good enough for Mom or Dad.

They went crazy. I couldn't even take in everything they were yelling about. Responsibility. Attitude. Punctuality. Consideration for others. Answering my phone whenever they call. I was trying to listen, but the only thing my brain could focus on was kissing Matt Parker. All I wanted to do was touch my lips and see what they felt like.

The yelling went on and on and on. Mom and Dad finally stopped, and we went to the dinner. But honestly, I don't understand why they were getting so upset. Gaga was celebrating her 79th birthday. After all that time, does starting an hour late make that much difference? And if we were so late, why were Mom and Dad wasting even more time yelling at me?

11:45 P.M.

I can't sleep. I can't stop thinking about kissing Matt Parker.

I close my eyes and pretend like I'm still kissing him. I want to be kissing him. I feel like I just drank ten Mocha Frappuccinos. I'm buzzing. I could be a poster girl for Starbucks. I could levitate. When Matt kissed me, it felt like something inside me changed. I think I look different. My fingers look longer, my nail beds look whiter, and my ankles slimmer. When I point my toes, I don't even feel like they're mine. My skin is sparkling. Is that possible?!

It sounds crazy! I sound crazy!

I keep thinking about Matt. I want to kiss him again.

Then I think about Brynn. I have to tell Brynn.

Then I think about Billy. For the first time since this afternoon, when I was going over to his house to find out why he's not talking to me, I think about Billy.

I'm just not sure what I think about Billy.

Love can sometimes be magic.

But magic can sometimes

just be an illusion.

—Javan, poet

Thursday, May 16
Study Hall
Pretending like everything's OK
But it's NOT

Telling Brynn what happened with Matt was a BIG mistake.

I thought maybe it would be another instance when she wouldn't say what she was thinking, but it wasn't. After homeroom, I told her what happened with Matt yesterday and she had a whole lot to say.

"How could you kiss Matt Parker? You barely

know him! What about Billy? How do you think Billy will feel after he kissed you, then you kissed Matt? Did you consider Billy's feelings?" I tried to explain to Brynn that I hadn't planned to kiss Billy or Matt, and that I had been on my way to try and find out what Billy's feelings were when Matt stopped me, showed me some pictures, and kissed me. But Brynn didn't want to hear any of my explanations.

She wanted to know if I'd thought about her feelings. She asked if I'd stopped for one second and thought about how it makes her feel that we're best friends and I've kissed two people before she's even kissed one. Then she asked what kind of friend it makes me that I would do that!

Brynn was making me feel like I should apologize for kissing two people who both technically kissed me. I tried to tell her I hadn't done anything to her, but Brynn was not in the mood to listen.

"You know, you're not my only best friend," she said. "Billy is my best friend too. And if he kissed any other girl and I found out she kissed another boy after he kissed her, I would tell him."

I froze. Sometimes I think being an only child, Brynn forgets the rules of sisterhood. I reminded her that she's like a sister to me and that when sisters tell each other their deepest secrets, they aren't supposed to share them with ANYBODY! Then I made Brynn promise she would never tell Billy that Matt and I kissed.

Brynn promised, but honestly, I wasn't convinced it was a promise she was going to keep. "Billy is probably thinking that the two of you are going to be boyfriend and girlfriend, which means you would have a boyfriend at camp," Brynn said. "Having a boyfriend at camp would be so much fun!" She asked me if I'd thought about that and said that if I had, she didn't see how I could have kissed Matt.

Then, Brynn said something I can't get out of my head. "I don't know if you've noticed, but Billy is the cutest guy in our grade and any girl would want him as her boyfriend."

She looked at me like it was my turn to say something. But I didn't know what to say. Part of me was thinking that Billy is cute and funny and sweet and smart, and having a boyfriend at camp would be fun. But another part of my brain, a big part, wasn't thinking about Billy. It was thinking about Brynn, and how she said that any girl in our grade would want Billy as a boyfriend, because what it made me think is:

Would Brynn?

5:15 P.M.
In my room

The rest of the school day was a disaster. Billy didn't speak to me, and Brynn could only talk about how I could have kissed Matt. When I told her I didn't want to talk about it anymore, she just rolled her eyes and shook her head like it would be hard to talk about anything else. The one person who did talk to me was Matt. When I passed him in the hall by the math classrooms, he stopped and made a joke about how certain things add up. But I freaked when I saw him and totally didn't get what he was saying, so all I did was ask if he'd made a bad grade on a test. He just shook his head and walked off.

OMG! What's wrong with me? I have to show Matt Parker I can be normal.

Mom just left to go to the diner. She said she has to go help Dad with something and she left me in charge of May and June. Since I'm the one in charge, I just told my little sisters to walk to Winn-Dixie to buy stuff to make s'mores. While they're gone, I'm going to drag out our fire pit and make a fire in it.

My plan is simple. My sisters will be gone long enough for me to get the fire started in the little part of my driveway that curves around behind the house, which you can't see from the street, but you can see from Matt's house. When Matt sees what I'm doing, he'll think it's cool and come over and hang out with me by the fire. Maybe he'll say something sweet about how girls in California never do cool things like make fires in their driveways. Can they even have driveway fires in California? Who knows? Who cares? Momentarily, Matt Parker and I will be snuggled up by the light of the fire.

Sometimes my sisters actually come in handy. If Mom hadn't asked me to babysit, I'd still be thinking about how I always say and do the stupidest things when Matt's around. But now I'm thinking about my genius plan.

6:02 P.M.
Fireside

It's a good thing I went to camp all those years. Otherwise I would have no clue what I'm doing. My fire is glowing nicely. All I have to do is wait.

6:12 P.M.
Still waiting

I look at my watch. I try to visualize sitting next to Matt at my driveway fire. I read in a magazine that the way to make things happen is to visualize them.

But the thing my brain keeps visualizing is sitting around a fire at camp next to Brynn and Billy. I've sat with them at dozens of campfires. I try to push all thoughts of them out of my head. I want to think about sitting next to Matt. It will be fun and cozy. Then, when my sisters are back, I'll get to eat s'mores, my all-time favorite food.

Matt Parker + s'mores = my definition of a perfect day. I'm just getting a little sick of waiting for perfection to begin.

6:42 p.m.
In my room
Where I will be for a long time
By choice

My parents are furious with me. I am more furious with them.

Obviously, some people do not know genius when they see it. My mother is one of those people. My father is another. While I was sitting around the fire, waiting for Matt Parker to come over, my parents pulled into the driveway. I have never seen parents look the way my parents looked. They were crazy-eyed, foaming at the mouth, rabid mad. I hope I never see anyone look like that ever again.

As they got out of the car, Mom was clutching May and June and a Winn-Dixie bag like they were precious little things (which, clearly, they are not, especially my sisters).

Dad slammed the driver's-side door so hard

the car was shaking. No kidding. When Dad saw the fire in the fire pit, he ran and grabbed the hose and sprayed the fire like he was putting out a wildfire.

Then he started yelling. My dad yelled so loud I'm sure anyone within a ten-mile radius (including Matt Parker) could hear.

He yelled for so long, I started to think I might be spending the rest of my teenage years in the driveway, with my dad yelling and my mother clutching my sisters and a shopping bag.

Here's the short version of what Dad had to say:

Could I imagine how it felt when my parents got a phone call at the diner that someone had found their two young daughters wandering the streets of Faraway? Two young girls, who I was supposed to be taking care of, were alone on a busy street. It was my job to protect them and keep them safe, and then what do my parents find when they come home? A fire in the driveway! My actions are grossly irresponsible!

Then Mom chimed in. Her face was all red and puffy. She honestly looked like she was having an allergic reaction. "April, your sisters could have been lost or hurt or even worse. You're going to be punished!"

But a) none of those things happened, and b) why am I going to be punished for not "taking care" of children who aren't even my children? I didn't have those children. I would never have had those children. God help me if I ever have children who turn out anything like my sisters.

I could sum this up in one word: OVER-REACTION! My parents should be embarrassed.

I'm supposed to be in my room thinking of a punishment that fits the crime. But I don't think I'm the one who deserves to be punished.

7:13 P.M.
Let the punishment fit the crime

I have thought of a punishment that fits the crime, and it's perfect.

The crime: My parents yelled at me, in public, with no regard for my feelings.

The punishment: I'm boycotting my parents. I won't look at them or talk to them. When they talk to me, I won't answer. When I want or need something, I will no longer use terms of endearment like Mom and Dad. From now on, I'm calling them Flora and Rex (but only when I want or need something). This punishment extends to any and all spawn of Flora and Rex Sinclair. Which means, in addition to boycotting my parents, I'm also boycotting my sisters. This punishment is to be enacted immediately and will cover the period of time from now until June 15, when I leave for camp. When I return home from camp four weeks later, I will consider revoking the punishment if, and only if, my parents and my sisters can treat me with the love and respect I deserve.

Hallelujah. I really am a genius.

10:14 P.M.

When my parents came in to tell me goodnight, my light was already off. I was waiting. I knew they'd come knocking. But I'm not talking. Not to them.

When Dad bent down and gave me a kiss on my forehead, I let out a loud pretend snore. Only thirty days till camp. I seriously can't wait.

Life is divided into

the horrible and the miserable.

—*Woody Allen*

Monday, May 20, 9:33 P.M.
Official worst day of my life

Why is this day different from all other days?

On all other days, I have something to look forward to. I have a reason to live.

But on this day, I do not. On this day, all my hopes and dreams and any excitement I had about life were squashed like a bug, because on this day my parents told me I'M NOT GOING TO CAMP! THEY HAVE MADE ALTER-NATE SUMMER PLANS FOR ME! THE

WORST PLANS I HAVE EVER HEARD OF!

I'm so upset I can hardly write. My tears are falling onto the page. My nose is red and puffy and more misshapen than ever. I'm not sure what cardiac arrest feels like, but I'm pretty sure I'm experiencing it. I want to curl up in a ball and die. I know that sounds dramatic but I don't care. The worst part is that I had no idea I was going to feel this way when I woke up this morning.

When I woke up, it seemed like today was going to be a great day.

When I went into the kitchen for breakfast, I didn't speak to anybody in my family. That's what I've been doing for four days now, and it has been going so well.

At school, I took two of my end-of-the-year exams, which I was totally prepared for. I'd had plenty of time over the weekend to study since I wasn't speaking to anyone in my family and neither of my best friends was saying much to me. My problems started when I walked into the house after school.

The minute I got home, I knew something was wrong. Mom and Dad were both sitting at the kitchen table. Mom hardly ever sits down unless she's sewing something, and there was no sewing machine in sight. And Dad is never at home in the middle of the afternoon. When I walked in, they had serious looks on their faces.

Dad asked me to please sit.

Since I'm not speaking to them, I didn't tell them sitting wasn't what I wanted to do. I handled it the way I've handled all direct requests from any of my family members since Thursday. I wrote my response, which was "No thank you," on a note card and held it up so they could see I wasn't planning to sit.

But that's when Dad pointed to a chair and told me to sit. He said it like he was talking to his dog, not his daughter. I knew I'd better sit, even though I didn't want to.

"April, Mom and I are very upset with your behavior and attitude lately." Dad started talking about how he and Mom don't like the way I've been acting since my birthday party.

Since I'm not talking to them, I didn't tell

them I don't like the way they've been acting since my birthday party either.

I thought Dad would be done after that, but he kept going. "Your mother and I see a negative pattern of behavior developing." He talked about how I made everyone late for Gaga's birthday dinner, and how I barely spoke to anyone the whole time I was there.

Since I'm not speaking to my parents, I didn't say that I didn't particularly want to talk to anyone at Gaga's birthday dinner and that I happened to have a whole lot of other things on my mind that night.

I rolled my eyes and looked at the kitchen clock like I had somewhere more important to be. I really thought Dad would take the hint and wrap it up at this point, but he kept going.

"The way you have been acting lately toward other members of this family is unacceptable." Dad brought up that I've been rude to him and mom and that I yell at my sisters.

If I had been speaking, what I would have told Dad is that I'm rude to him and mom because they say annoying things and make me do stuff I don't want to do and that I yell at my sisters because they do all kinds of things they shouldn't do to me, including but not limited to taking my stuff, sneaking into my room, and using my phone for what could easily be classified as child pornography.

He went on about how I "irresponsibly" sent them off to buy groceries and made a fire in the driveway. If you ask me, what Dad should have been doing was thanking me for babysitting them in the first place.

I REALLY thought Dad should be done at this point, but he was still going strong.

He talked about how I haven't spoken to anyone in this family for days. How it's "completely unacceptable." He said I seem disconnected from this family and that's not good for anyone, particularly me.

I didn't think I should have to explain to Dad that being disconnected from this family is great for me and that I've never been happier. I just sat there with my arms crossed, looking at my parents. I couldn't imagine that there was anything else Dad could possibly say. If I'd had another note card on me, I would have written, "Are we done yet?"

But I didn't have a note card. And it wouldn't have mattered anyway.

Dad was SO not done.

That's when he looked at Mom, and Mom looked at him, and they did this weird nod like it was time. Then Dad looked at me and said the six words that ruined my life. "April, you're not going to camp."

After that, everything was a blur. Dad said all this stuff about how I need to re-bond (which I don't even think is a word) with him and Mom and my sisters. He said that with every right comes responsibility, and as a member of this family, it is my responsibility to conduct myself in an "appropriate manner." He said that it will also be my responsibility to babysit my sisters this summer when school is out. Then he said that he and mom bought an RV and that we're taking a two-week family vacation in it to Florida as part of the re-bonding process.

When I heard all this, I ended my boycott. "ARE YOU SERIOUS?!" I screamed. I've never been so mad in my life. I told them it's unfair to blame me for having bad behavior when the problems start with everyone else. I told them that I am just reacting to how horribly they are all acting. I told them that I am a teenager now and they need to start treating me like one. I told them that they can't just give me respon- sibilities when I have ABSOLUTELY NO RIGHTS AT ALL!

But no matter what I said, my parents wouldn't change their minds.

I even reminded Dad (who shouldn't have needed reminding) that he just opened a new restaurant. "Can you really afford to leave the diner for two whole weeks?" I asked. I thought I was making a very smart business point and that Dad would see the logic in that and change his mind, but all he did was ramble on about family priorities and his highly capable assistant manager.

Then he told me the conversation was over and camp was out. He'd already called the di- rector. I was staying home.

In my thirteen years of life, this was categorically the worst moment ever. I started begging. I literally got down on my knees and begged my parents to let me go to camp. I begged and I cried and I told them my heart would break in two if my friends left for camp without me.

But my parents didn't care. They just sat there like nothing I could say or do would make them change their minds.

So I told my parents if they didn't let me go to camp, I would run away from home.

Dad said if I wanted to do that, he would give me a thousand dollars, but if I took the money I could never come back. It was the most insane, stupid, heartless thing I could imagine a parent saying to a kid. I'm going to remember it forever and never say anything like that to my own kids. I'm seriously scarred for life.

Now I'm in my room, where I've been since I had this miserable talk with my parents. I haven't stopped crying. I haven't had anything to eat or drink since lunch. The only person who has even come to check on me is May, who said she just wanted to know if I'm going to stay or take the thousand dollars and leave. She asked if she could have my room if I go.

I hate my life. I really do.

I have nothing more to say.

There is nothing more to say.

I've developed a new philosophy: I only dread one day at a time.

—Charlie Brown

Tuesday, May 21

Depressed

I'm depressed. I told Brynn my parents won't let me go to camp.

I thought it would make me feel better to tell her, but it made me feel worse. Brynn just kept saying how it's the most unbelievable thing she'd ever heard, and she'd kill her parents if they did something like that to her. She said she can't imagine what it will be like to be at camp with Billy and without me. That was not what I was hoping she'd say.

I can't even write. I'm too depressed.

Wednesday, May 22
More depressed

I'm even more depressed today than I was yesterday.

Billy and I finally talked today. That sounds like a good thing, but it wasn't. Billy talked to me because Brynn told him I told her that my parents won't let me go to camp. He said it was too bad, but I didn't know if he meant it's too bad for me that I don't get to go or that it's too bad for him because he wishes I were going. So I asked him, and that's when our talk turned into a fight. Our first big fight ever.

Billy didn't want to talk about camp—he wanted to talk about kissing. He asked me if I told Brynn he kissed me.

I didn't want to lie, and it seemed like he knew the answer anyway.

When I told him I had, he said all kinds of stuff about how he couldn't believe I would tell Brynn and that he thought I should know that he wouldn't want me to, and how he trusted me not to tell anyone, but that was a mistake.

I tried to apologize, but Billy didn't want to hear anything I had to say. And now we're not talking. Again.

I'm upset that Billy and I aren't talking, but I don't know why. Things are no different now than before we started talking today anyway.

Thursday, May 23
Still depressed

It's the next-to-last day of school. All we did in school was eat doughnuts and sign yearbooks. I should be happy, but I'm not.

Friday, May 24
Last day of school
Last bell just rang
Last student to leave
(i.e., me)

Question: What's worse than the school year?

Answer: Summer break.

But only if your name is April Sinclair and you have the summer ahead of you that I have.

I've never been so unexcited about school ending in my entire life.

One more question: Where's the nearest supply closet? I'd like to hide in it until next fall.

Tuesday, June 11
I think
I'm not sure
I don't know
I don't care

I haven't written anything for a long time, because I haven't had anything good to write about. I've been forced to spend large amounts of time with people (my sisters) I have absolutely no desire to spend time with.

I haven't seen Matt. For all I know he moved back to California.

Billy hasn't spoken to me since our fight, and I still don't know why. I don't know if it's because he's mad I told Brynn or confused about how he felt when he kissed me or upset he kissed me in the first place.

I completely don't get what's going on. All I know is that I miss talking to Billy, partly because I just miss Billy, but also because it means that the only other people I talk to who are anywhere near my age are May and June, who I don't like talking to, and Brynn, who only talks about a camp I'm not going to.

June 14, 9:45 P.M.
Staring at an empty duffle

June 14 was supposed to be the day when I would pack my duffle bag, because tomorrow is June 15, the day I was supposed to leave for camp.

It's making me sick that I'm not going. My stomach is upset and my head aches and my feet hurt. I feel like I'm getting one of those diseases people get when their life is too sad for them to lead a healthy existence.

I hate my parents for making me stay home. I'm too young to be filled with this kind of hatred.

And I know that as depressed as I am now, it won't compare to how depressed I'll be tomorrow morning at 6:45 A.M. when my friends are on their way to Camp Silver Shores and I'm stuck at home.

I'm not a happy camper.

Saturday, June 15, 7:30 A.M.
Went to the bus to say good-bye
Back in bed
Tears on my pillow

I set my alarm for 6:30 so I could go to Far-away Middle School and say goodbye to my friends before they got on the bus. But I should have stayed in bed.

When Brynn saw me, she gave me a big hug and said she was going to miss me sooooo much and that camp wouldn't be nearly as much fun without me, but I don't think she meant it because she was hugging everybody and scream-ing about how much fun camp would be.

I saw Billy too. Since he's leaving for a while, I thought he might say something like, *April, I'm sorry things got so messed up between us. I really like you and I'm glad I kissed you. Camp won't be the same without you, and don't worry, I'll write.*

But he didn't say anything like that. He didn't say anything at all. Not even good-bye. It was really weird. When I told him, "Bye and have fun," he just looked at me like he was going to say something, but he didn't.

Then he and Brynn got on the bus with twenty-eight other screaming kids.

I watched as thirty screaming kids in Camp Silver Shores T-shirts drove off. But there should have been thirty-one kids on that bus.

Two cannibals are eating a clown. One says to the other, "Does this taste funny to you?"

Sunday, June 16, 5:30 P.M.

Since I woke up this morning, I've watched seven episodes of *Real Housewives of New Jersey* and eaten an entire shoebox of Life cereal. Why a shoebox? Because all the cereal in our house ends up in shoeboxes under May's bed where she keeps it in case she gets hungry in the middle of the night.

While my friends are eating roasted marshmallows and singing songs around a fire, I'm stuck eating cereal out of a shoebox and watching a bunch of ladies scream at each other on TV.

Mom just came into my room to check on me. When she did, I made the saddest face I could possibly make. I thought there was a chance she would say something about how she's already starting to realize she and Dad made a big mistake. But all she said was that I shouldn't worry, that this summer will be good for me.

I fail to see how.

Monday, June 17, 6:50 A.M.

It's 6:50 in the morning and I'm listening to my dad yelling, "Paper, Gilligan. Paper!"

My dad been has been standing in our front yard in his robe and slippers yelling for Gilligan to get the newspaper for at least 20 minutes. He's determined to train Gilligan to fetch the paper. Gilligan seems determined not to learn. In the amount of time my dad has been yelling, he could have gotten the paper himself and read the thing front to back.

And Dad doesn't just yell like a normal person yelling to a dog. He yells in a wake-up-the-whole-neighborhood kind of way. It's completely embarrassing.

It's also exhausting. I just walked outside and told Dad that as a result of being awakened so early, I will NOT be able to perform my job duties today, which he and Mom have defined as making lunch for my sisters and keeping them entertained this afternoon. Dad replied with some stupid comment about the early bird getting the worm.

I didn't see what the early bird had to do with any of this, but I asked Dad if while the early bird was out getting the worm, he could get the paper too.

I thought that was pretty funny. But Dad didn't see the humor. He said I should try to be more "respectful." I told Dad I should be at camp where my "lack of respect" wouldn't bother him.

Dad didn't think that was funny either.

Tuesday, June 18

I have nothing to write about.

Here's what I will be doing today, which

also happens to be what I did yesterday: making lunch for my sisters and keeping them entertained. In fact, I will be doing this every day this week, so if I write nothing else, it's because I already know I will have ABSOLUTELY NOTHING TO WRITE ABOUT.

Thursday, June 20

Hallelujah! Tomorrow I will have something to write about. Mom said I can take May and June to the pool to swim.

Friday, June 21, 3:50 p.m.
The Ultimate Embarrassment
The kind you never recover from

Unfortunately, today I have something to write about. This afternoon I took May and June to the pool, which I was looking forward to, but what happened there was so humiliating, I'm certain beyond a reasonable doubt that I'll never be the same again.

It pains me to write about it, but here goes.

After lunch, May and June and I walked to the pool. I was really excited. I had on my new bikini that I had to beg Mom to buy for me. It has removable pads, so I took out the right pad, which made my boobs look the same size. I thought I actually looked good.

When we got to the pool, I swam with May and June for a while. We had fun. They were really good and listened to everything I told them. When we were done swimming, I took them to the snack bar and we all got frozen candy bars and Cokes. Everything was going great. Then Matt Parker came over to the snack bar.

I didn't even know he was at the pool. With the exception of the one time in the hallway at school, I haven't seen him since we kissed. It's like he disappeared and suddenly reappeared. That's when the most embarrassing moment of my entire life happened. Here's a recap:

Matt: (Looking totally hot) Hey April, what's up?
Me: (Trying to look and sound cool) Not much.
Matt: (Smiling) I like your bikini.
Me: (Smiling and about to say something cool and/or funny and/or clever, but didn't have a chance to because my crazy sister said something

first.)

June: It's a string bikini. That's what April calls it.

Matt: (Still smiling) I see that.

June: (Putting her hands on her hips.) It's got strings here.

Matt: (Still smiling) I see that.

June: And there's another string down there.

The next thing I knew, June was pointing to my crotch. I looked down. The end of my tampon string was hanging out, and Matt Parker was standing there staring at it. I swatted June away, but it was too late. Matt started laughing hysterically and looked away. Then, before I could even finish grabbing my towel to wrap around my waist, he said something about having to go, and he was out of sight.

I thought I was going to die of embarrassment. I wanted to die.

I STILL WANT TO DIE.

Houston, we have a problem.

—Apollo 13

Still Saturday, June 22
9:44 P.M.

I have a large problem, and it's not that Matt Parker knows I'm having my period.

When I went to the mailbox this afternoon to get the mail, I came to the horrible realization that Billy and Brynn have been at camp for a week and I haven't gotten a letter from either one of them. I've been spending so much time in babysitting hell, I haven't had time to think about my friends, but now I'm fully focused and I have some questions. First up on my list: Why haven't I heard from Brynn?

Given everything that's happened with Billy, I didn't expect to get a letter from him, but no mail from Brynn?! She's been at camp for a whole week, and I don't think it's too much to expect a letter, one stupid letter, from my best friend. What's going on at Camp Silver Shores that's making Brynn Stephens too busy to write to her best friend?

I don't want to think about why Brynn hasn't written, but what I'm starting to think is this: Brynn + Billy together at camp without me = not a good thing.

People get really close at camp. They're already close, but I know they're going to get even closer just like the three of us do every summer. Without me there, the two of them will be like twins who tell each other everything.

Billy will tell Brynn that he's mad at me for telling her he kissed me. Brynn, who said, "Any girl would want Billy for a boyfriend," which I can't help but think includes her, will tell him that I kissed Matt, and then she will snag Billy for herself. She's the one who said it would be so much fun to have a boyfriend at camp. Even though I'm not sure I want Billy for a boyfriend, I know I don't want Brynn to have him.

Sunday, June 23, 2:15 P.M.
At my desk

If Brynn isn't writing to me, I'm going to write to her, and then she'll have to write back.

2:55 P.M.

I just wrote to Brynn. The only problem is that today is Sunday, and there are only five days before we leave on our family RV pilgrimage to Florida on Friday.

I don't want to go to Florida with no letter in hand. Actually, I don't want to go to Florida at all. But that's a different story.

I'm going to put my trust in the only place I can think to put it: the United States Postal Service.

Monday, June 24, 4:45 P.M.

No mail from Brynn.

Tuesday, June 25, 4:53 p.m.

Where's my letter postmarked from Camp Silver Shores?

Wednesday, June 26, 4:59 p.m.
Standing outside by the mailbox

The postman just delivered our mail and there was NOTHING for me. Was it too much to ask that he deliver one little envelope with my name on it?

I'm sure he's a nice guy, but right now, the postman is not on my top-ten list.

Thursday, June 27, 5:18 p.m.

Good news: the mail arrived. Bad news: There was none for me.

No letter from Brynn, and I'm leaving in the morning to go to Florida for two weeks. How am I supposed to enjoy my vacation when I have no idea what my friends are doing behind my back? How do I even know they're still my friends?

5:32 P.M.

My life continues to spiral downhill. Dad just drove into our driveway in an old, dilapidated camper. He calls it an RV. I'm calling it the Clunker.

I can't believe he actually thinks this vehicle will make it to Florida and back.

5:44 P.M.

I don't think Dad thinks this vehicle will make it to Florida and back. I just heard him tell Mom it doesn't look anything like the picture on the Internet.

7:42 P.M.

Mom just told me to start packing.

Dad said we're leaving at 4 A.M. When I asked him why we have to leave at 4 in the morning, he said, "To get a jump on the day."

I asked why we would want to get a jump on the day.

He said he shouldn't have to answer that question.

Translation: THERE IS NO ANSWER!

Remember. As far as anyone knows,

we're a nice normal family.

—*Homer Simpson*

Friday, June 28, 4:07 A.M.
That's right, A.M.!

I fail to see the normalcy in anything my family does. It's 4:07 A.M. and we're in the Clunker, hurtling toward Florida. Three cities. Fourteen days. Countless amusement parks.

I am not amused.

8:30 A.M.
Sitting at the table in a moving vehicle
Playing Go Fish with young children
I'm pretty sure what I've endured for the

last four and a half hours qualifies as kidnapping. Being forced into a vehicle against my will. Not allowed to exit. Made to play games well below my intellectual and emotional level. Only given doughnuts as nourishment.

If the United States Government really wanted to punish terrorists, they'd round them up and make them come on this vacation with us. Not only would they have to deal with the intolerable conditions mentioned above, they'd also have to endure Dad's terrible driving. He says he's just getting the feel of the thing. I say we're one turn away from toppling over. Every time Dad goes left or right, all the cards go flying. Dad keeps making the same joke about playing fifty-two-card pickup. May and June think it's hilarious. I don't see the humor in any of this.

We don't even get to stop and use the bathroom. WHY? Because the Clunker has its own bathroom! Dad says we're only stopping for gas. He wants to make it to St Augustine by noon. And once we get there, guess what we're doing.

Parking the Clunker on a campsite for clunkers and sleeping in it.

We're stopping for gas soon. I'm thinking of making a run for it.

9:16 A.M.

We just stopped for gas. I thought about running, but there was nowhere to go. As far as the eye could see, there were only trees and cows.

9:43 A.M.

I'm bored.

I'm sick of sitting at a table with my sisters, eating doughnuts, and playing Go Fish. I'm going to go lie down in the bedroom, which is just a raised platform with a thin mattress on top and a curtain around it. I'm going to try to go to sleep and maybe when I wake up, I'll find out this whole thing was just a nightmare.

10:48 A.M.

I'm awake. I slept one for one lousy hour. But now, on top of being bored and miserable,

I'm also nauseous. I asked Dad if we could stop so I could throw up, but he said we have a toilet on board that will work just fine.

10:54 A.M.

I forgot to mention that I'm also hot. Dad said there must be a problem with the air conditioning. For once, I agree with my father.

1:46 P.M.

We're now at the campground where we're parking the Clunker and sleeping for the next three nights while we're in St. Augustine, Florida. Dad said, "We've arrived at Florida's finest." June seemed to like those words because she's been repeating them nonstop ever since he said them. She said it sounds like a tongue twister and she wanted to see how many times she could say, "We've arrived at Florida's finest." May said they should make it a challenge to see who could say it more times, so they've been continuously repeating what Dad said ever since we got here. Mom just looked at me and said I should join in the fun.

I told Mom I'd be happy to do that if there was anything here that looked like fun.

She replied that I need to work on my attitude.

4:25 P.M.
A crappy situation

I wish there was a ladylike way to say what I'm about to say, but there's not. So here goes: Dad spent the afternoon getting rid of the pee and poop in our RV.

It sounds just as gross as it is. First Dad had to find the "disposal site" where he could put our "waste products." I told May and June that was just a fancy name for a hole in the ground where you put your crap. June kept asking Dad if he'd found the hole in the ground for the crap. Dad got mad at me for teaching June the word *crap*. He also got sweaty because it took him a long time to find the hole and it was really hot outside.

I tried to suggest to Dad that he should come inside the RV and cool down. But then I reminded him that our air conditioner wasn't working so that wasn't really an option. Dad didn't seem to appreciate that reminder. He said he could only deal with one RV issue at a time.

Anyway, once Dad found the hole, he put on these thick rubber gloves. They made him look like an unlicensed dentist or a child molester, and I told him so, but he said he didn't want to hear another word from me. Then he started mumbling some weird stuff about needing to find the sewer hose compartment. I thought I was hearing things.

Who goes on vacation looking for a sewer hose compartment?

Once Dad found the compartment, he took a hose out of our camper and stuck it in the hole in the ground. Then he opened up some sort of flap and all the pee and poop from our camper started going through the hose and into the hole. Dad stood there holding the hose in his gloved hands saying how he had to do this until it fully drained.

That's an image I didn't need. No one wants to see their dad with his hands around a sewage hose waiting for it to drain.

And it gets worse. When Dad was done, he washed off his gloves and said he was saving them for next time. I'm horribly grossed out. I'm also completely unclear as to why my parents thought this trip would bring me closer to my family.

I've never wanted to get farther away!

Sunday morning, June 30, 8:45 A.M.

Going to Florida is every kid's dream, but to be honest, I don't get the attraction. For the past two days, all we've done is look at old stuff in St. Augustine, which Mom says is the oldest city in America. We saw an old school. An old house. An old fort. An old museum. An old jail. An old cemetery. They even have people here who dress up in old clothes to make you feel like you're taking a trip back in time.

May and June were taking a bunch of pictures, and they actually thought it was fun seeing everything. But I didn't. Which part of teenagers-are-into-new-stuff don't my parents understand? It seems like Mom and Dad made me come on this trip so our family could "re-bond," yet they've planned nothing in the way of activities that I feel has been helpful to this process.

I don't get it. They're so weird (my parents), and they made such weird children (my sisters), and they make such weird choices (purposely taking a vacation to the oldest city in America).

I sincerely hope this trip improves, and SOON!

8:30 P.M.
Just finished another day of sightseeing

I'd like to write that today was fun, but it wasn't. We went to an alligator farm, a pirate museum, and to see the Fountain of Youth. When the guy who works at the fountain asked if I'd like to taste the water, I said what I'd really like was a Diet Snapple. Mom and Dad failed to see the humor. I thought it was funny, and for just a minute it made me stop thinking about Brynn and Billy and what they're doing at camp without me, which is what I'd been thinking about pretty much the whole day.

We leave tomorrow for Disney World, which I hope will be more fun than where we've been. (It won't be hard to beat.)

It always looks darkest

before it gets totally black.

—*Charlie Brown*

Monday, July 1
In the parking lot of Disney World

The good news: We made it to Disney World.

The bad news: The bottom fell out the minute we arrived. The bottom of the Clunker literally fell out and bits and pieces of it are all over the Disney World parking lot. When it was happening, I thought there was an earthquake. I'm not sure if they have earthquakes in Florida (and I definitely didn't think they have them at Disney World), but what they do have here is a lot of sunshine and heat. We've been standing in it for over two hours waiting for the mechanic to get here. While throngs of other people are going into amusement parks filled with countless fun things to do, we're stuck in a parking lot.

Monday, July 1, 10:30 P.M.
At the Contemporary Hotel
Official worst day of my life

I've said it before, but this time I mean it. Today was truly the worst day of my life. I didn't think things could get any worse on this trip, but they did. They got much worse.

Here's what happened.

While we were waiting in the parking lot for the mechanic to arrive, Dad finally decided that it was stupid for all of us to be standing there, so Mom took May and June and me into the Magic Kingdom while Dad stayed back to deal with the Clunker.

Inside the Magic Kingdom, we went on a bunch of rides, and Mom bought May and June matching hats with Mickey Mouse ears on them. They were excited about their hats, but all I could think about was how everything we were doing was too babyish for me. It seemed like once again, Mom was just thinking about May and June and not what I would like.

By dinnertime, Dad was still dealing with the Clunker, so Mom took us to get something to eat. We'd just finished dinner and were walking around Main Street when Mom's cell phone rang. It was Dad calling to tell her what was going on with the Clunker, so Mom asked me if I would take May and June into the gift shop and watch them while she was on the phone with Dad. What was going through my head was that I didn't know why we had to come all the way to Florida for me to babysit my sisters, when that's what I've been doing all summer at home. After everything that happened today, it makes me sick that that's what I was thinking.

Anyway, I took May and June into the gift shop, and I started looking for presents for Brynn and Billy. I didn't know if Billy was going to want a present from me, but I figured I'd better get him one just in case. And I definitely needed to get something for Brynn. I started looking in the jewelry aisle, and I told May and June to stay there with me. There was a lot to look at, and I guess I got kind of caught up in looking for the right gifts, because the next time I looked up, there was no sign of May or June anywhere.

I told myself to stay calm. They had to be somewhere nearby. I started looking all over the gift store. I was calling out their names, but no one answered. I felt a knot forming in my stomach. They were nowhere in the gift shop.

I knew I needed to stay calm, but I was starting to feel way too hot. Everything around me seemed to be getting blurry. I had to find my sisters. Even though Mom was the last person I wanted to find out that I'd lost May and June, I knew I had to find her.

I went out of the gift store and saw Mom sitting on a bench. She was still on her phone. I could feel beads of sweat running down my face as I walked towards her. When I told her I couldn't find May and June, the look on her face was the worst I've ever seen.

"April, you were supposed to be watching

your sisters!" Mom looked like she was going to be sick. I felt sick too. One minute my sisters were right beside me, and the next minute they were gone, and it was my fault.

Mom grabbed my arm, and we started running up and down Main Street looking for May and June. We were calling their names, but there was no sign of them anywhere.

It was terrible. Main Street was jam-packed with people. We could hardly see around the crowds. A few times I thought I saw May and June in their Mickey Mouse ears, but it was other little kids in the same hats. Other kids, other sisters, who were safe with their families and having fun.

As we pushed past people, yelling for my sisters, everyone was looking at us like they felt sorry for us, like no one would want to lose a kid among all these thousands of people. I didn't think it was possible, but their looks made me feel even worse.

A security officer heard us yelling and came over to help. He asked us all kinds of questions. Names. Clothing. Interests. He wanted to know everything about May and June. Mom was showing him pictures on her cell phone of what they look like.

It was starting to get dark.

The security officer called a bunch of other security officers and they all spread out, calling May and June's names. I started crying. Everyone was yelling and looking.

My sisters were lost and it was because I wasn't watching them when I should have been. I was trying to stay focused on the search, but my brain was thinking so many horrible thoughts. What if something terrible happened to my sisters? What if someone bad took them? What if they wandered into the inner workings of one of the rides and got hurt? What if we never found them? What if I ended up as an only child?

I kept looking at Mom, who was a weird shade of white and more serious than I'd ever seen her. I couldn't bear to think about how my parents would feel if something happened to May and June.

Mom and I kept looking in all the restaurants and shops on Main Street. There was so much Disney paraphernalia everywhere, but the only thing I wanted to see were my sisters' little faces.

It felt like we had been looking for so long, and my brain was completely filled with the fear that they were lost for good.

Mom and I had just looked for the third time inside an old-fashioned ice-cream shop when I heard someone screaming my name from the street. I ran outside, and there was June sitting on May's shoulders, screaming my name. At first I wondered if I was seeing things, but as they walked toward me in their Mickey Mouse ears, I knew it was real. Mom and I ran over to them and hugged them both. The security officers came over to make sure everyone was OK.

Normally, I would have gotten mad at them for leaving the gift shop and not listening to me when I told them to stay near me, but I was so happy to see them both that all I could do was hug them and cry. Mom was crying too. Neither one of us could stop until June told us it was her idea for May to put June on her shoulders so she could see over the crowd and find me. Then

May gave us a demonstration of how she bent down so June could climb on her shoulders, and how she used all of her strength to stand up. I hugged them both really tight again. I told June I was proud of her for coming up with such a smart idea, and I told May I was proud of her for being so strong.

The rest of the evening was a blur. We went to a hotel where Dad had gotten us rooms because, as he said, "The Clunker is officially dead. R.I.P."

I spent most of tonight apologizing for what happened and for not watching May and June more closely. But the truth is, my apologies feel worthless when I think what could have happened to my sisters. Mom and Dad had a very long talk with me about responsibility, kind of like the Winn-Dixie day talk, although this one was different because I agreed with everything they said. I told them there's no punishment they could give me that would be worse than the idea of something bad having happened to my sisters. And I meant it.

I'm just glad they're safe. It's been a long day

and I'm glad it's over. I'm glad to be going to sleep in a room with my sisters. And I'd be lying if I said that I wasn't particularly glad this room is air-conditioned.

Wednesday, July 3, 4:17 P.M.
In our room

Two days. Four parks. Five roller coasters. One safari. A jungle trek. A musical. And too many other rides, pins, and autographs to even count. My brain is fried, but in a good way.

Dad just came back to the room. He was in the lobby for a long time renting a car and booking hotel rooms for the rest of our trip.

He seemed very tired, so I offered to take May and June to the lobby to buy some candy and babysit while he and Mom take a nap. He said to keep a close eye on them.

I assured him that would not be a problem.

6:17 P.M.
A fun afternoon with my sisters!
Did I just write that? I did!

It feels totally strange to write that I had a

good time with my sisters, but I actually did. And I'm not saying that just because I feel bad (which I still do) about losing them the other day.

When May and June and I went to the lobby to buy candy, May saw some kids throwing Jelly Bellies at each other and decided we should too. I said it sounded like fun, and June said it would be even more fun if we did it from a high floor in our hotel, which has hallways around each floor and a big, open atrium in the middle with lots of people wandering around in the lobby below.

So May and June and I bought a bag of Jelly Bellies and went up to the 5th floor and started throwing them at people in the lobby. Every time we'd throw a Jelly Belly and hit somebody, we'd duck down behind the balcony ledge so no one in the lobby would know where the Jelly Bellies were coming from, and then we'd laugh hysterically. In addition to having super-human strength, May also has amazing aim, so she did most of the throwing. She didn't throw hard enough to hurt anybody, but it was enough to make them jump.

I know throwing Jelly Bellies at people is wrong, and I feel badly saying this, but laughing and throwing Jelly Bellies at people with my sisters was a lot of fun.

When we finished, we sat down on the floor of the hallway and fed each other the rest of the Jelly Bellies and tried to guess the flavors. After that, I took May and June to the pool at our hotel, and then we went on the Monorail, an elevated train that took us all over Disney World. It was amazing. We could see the parks and rides and hotels and people out the window.

When we got back to our hotel, May and June held my hands on the way back to the room. It was like a really cheesy moment from a made-for-TV movie where something bad happens to a family then everyone gets really close. But the truth is . . . it was sweet.

Happy July 4!
9:15 A.M.
Cinderella's Castle

We just ate breakfast at Cinderella's castle. June waited around for a really long time to get

Cinderella's autograph, and when she got it, she gave it to me and said she wanted me to have it.

Honestly, I really don't care about Cinderella's autograph, but I knew how much it meant to June. So I told her we could keep it in a safe place in her room and that it would belong to both of us.

Mom told me she was proud of me for handling the situation in such a mature way.

It was weird to hear her say that. But weird in a good way.

Well, I must be off for another amusing day. Ha! Amusement parks. Amusing. Sometimes I crack myself up.

10:55 P.M.
In our room
Fun day
Lots of rides
Lots of fireworks

Tonight we saw the biggest, most awesome fireworks show ever. There was red, white, and blue everywhere you looked. It had music, too.

I hate to say it, but it was even bigger and

more awesome than the fireworks over Silver Lake at camp.

Whoa . . . camp. Fireworks. Friends. My brain hadn't thought about all that for what feels like a long time. I don't think there was anything good about losing my little sisters on vacation, but it did make me forget about all the stuff I'm usually obsessed with.

Even though part of me can't help thinking about Billy and Brynn and wondering what's going on at camp without me, part of me is glad to be where I am.

Friday, July 5, 10:45 p.m.
In our room
Last night at Disney World

Another fun day of rides and slides. We went to a water park called Blizzard Beach that was so cool. Literally. It was like being in a blizzard and at the beach at the same time. We went down a bunch of water slides, and we went rafting and tobogganing too. We even got to go on a chair-lift like the kind they have at ski resorts.

May kept trying to pick people up when they

came off the chair lift. When she started doing it, I told her to stop because it was embarrassing. Then I decided to let her do whatever she wanted because I didn't know anyone anyway. The funny thing is that when I stopped telling her not to pick people up, she stopped picking people up.

Tonight is our last night here. Tomorrow morning, we leave for the Florida Keys to go snorkeling for four days. I have to admit that what started out as the worst trip ever has had its moments. And by that, shockingly, I mean good ones.

*Don't tell me the moon
is shining. Show me the glint
of light on broken glass.*

—*Anton Chekov*

Tuesday, July 9, 5:45 P.M.
Key Largo, Florida
In a hammock
On the beach

I can't believe we've been snorkeling in the
Florida Keys for the last four days. And what I
really can't believe is that we have to go home
tomorrow.

It's too bad because I like it here.

I'd like it a whole lot more if Dad would stop
saying annoying stuff like, "It's so nice to have
the old April back." And, "I knew this trip was

a good idea."

But whatever. I'd never snorkeled before this trip, and it's definitely one of the coolest things I've ever done. If I was old enough to drive (and if I had a car), I'd get a bumper sticker that says I LOVE SNORKELING.

The first day we got here, Mom and Dad bought us a bunch of equipment for snorkeling. Masks. Snorkels. Fins. Mom made a video of May and June and me trying out our equipment on the beach. I knew we looked funny walking around like we couldn't find the ocean, but I didn't care. I put on the fins and mask and pretended like I was a sea monster and chased June around the beach. She was laughing so hard. It was really funny.

Once we got the hang of how the equipment worked, we practiced snorkeling in shallow water. We learned how to breathe through the snorkel and float on our stomachs with fins on.

Then we practiced diving under the surface of the water. We started off still in shallow water. You could see fish and plants under the water that you would never know existed if you hadn't looked under the surface. But snorkeling near the shore couldn't compare to the snorkeling we did during the rest of the trip.

For the last three days, we've gotten to go on snorkel boats and explore the only living coral barrier reef in North America.

The first day we went, the boat captain gave us a quick course on what to do. He gave us some rules: Don't feed the fish. Don't touch the coral. If you see sea turtles or dolphins, don't touch them.

Then he taught us some hand signals to use under water. Stuff like: I've had enough and I'm doing fine.

He said we'd also be doing a lot of signaling for other people to take a look at the cool stuff we'd be seeing. And he was right. What I've seen under water is so completely cool—tons of tropical coral formations, and underwater plants, and all kinds of colorful fish.

Our boat captain told us we were seeing the third largest coral reef in the world, and that the corals had been there for 5,000 to 7,000 years.

When I was in St. Augustine, I didn't like

looking at things that were hundreds of years old. Change of opinion: old stuff can be pretty cool after all.

Seeing everything underwater was amazing, but the best part about being under the surface of the ocean was how it felt to be part of an underwater world that I never knew existed. It seemed incredible that I spend every day at school, in my room, hanging out with my friends . . . while there's a whole other world filled with things that had been there for thousands of years that I didn't know about before this trip.

This sounds weird, but snorkeling made me think that the world is full of things I don't know about yet. Things I've never thought about before or even known to think about. And just realizing that made me happy. Everything underwater was so quiet and relaxing and beautiful. I felt like I could have stayed down there just looking at the fish and corals forever.

But as Dad said, all good things must end.

And that's exactly what's happening tomorrow.

Hi-ho, hi-ho. Back to Faraway we go.

I never thought I'd say this (and I certainly

wouldn't say it to my parents), but this trip has been pretty good.

10:30 P.M.

The other thing I've done a lot of on this trip besides snorkeling is eating key lime pie. It's my new favorite food (right up there with s'mores). Dad likes it too. He's taking home a bag of key limes, and he's going to find a recipe so he can start to serve key lime pie at the Love Doctor Diner.

Who knows? I just might start wanting to eat there.

Sometimes the questions

are complicated and

the answers are simple.

—*Dr. Seuss*

Thursday, July 11, 3:45 P.M.
An unopened letter in my hand
Lots of unanswered questions in my head

Going away with my family turned out to be good in ways I hadn't imagined. It made me forget about all the things I was stressing about before the trip.

Kissing Billy. Kissing Matt. Telling Brynn. Fighting with Billy. Wondering if Matt likes me. Trying to figure out how I feel about Matt. Trying to figure out how I feel about Billy. Hoping Brynn isn't getting together with Billy at camp while I'm at home.

That's all I thought about before we left. But during the trip, at least after the first few days, all I thought about were water parks, roller coasters, and tropical fish. It kind of felt like a relief to leave my normal life behind and do things like eat Jelly Bellies in the hallway of a hotel with my sisters.

But it's weird now, because the minute Mom handed me the letter I got from Brynn while I was gone, it's like I never left.

I'm a little scared to open her letter. I feel like the minute I do, I'm going to find out things I'm not sure I want to know. Things like: Are Billy and Brynn having fun together without me at camp? Did Brynn tell Billy what happened with Matt? She swore she wouldn't, but did they bond over a campfire and start talking? Are Brynn and Billy a couple? Are we still the Three Musketeers, or are they now two Reese's Peanut Butter Cups who belong in the same package, and I'm the lone Hershey Bar?

I guess it's time to find out.

4:07 P.M.

The only thing I found out was who won the color war.

Reading a letter that doesn't tell you what you want to know, even if you weren't sure you wanted to know it, is worse than reading no letter at all. It makes you sure you want to know what you weren't sure you wanted to know. AND I WANT TO KNOW WHAT'S GOING ON AT CAMP SILVER SHORES!

Billy and Brynn don't come home until Saturday, and I don't know how I'm going to be able to wait until then to find out.

4:23 P.M.

Mom is doing the laundry. May and June are watching TV. Dad went to the diner. All I'm doing is sitting here wondering what my friends are doing.

I have to find something else to do.

4:49 P.M.

I'm going to walk Gilligan. It's not what I want to do, but it's the only thing I can think to do. I hope walking Gilligan will help me stop wondering what my friends are doing.

OMG! I'm back from walking Gilligan, and I'm wondering so many more things than I was wondering before I went on the walk and saw Matt Parker.

He didn't see me, because I hid behind some trees in Dr. Blackwell's yard. But I saw him, and he wasn't alone. He was with Jillian Diamond, eighth-grade drama queen, both on the stage and off. I could hear them laughing, and he was giving her a piggy back ride. No joke. She was on his back with her arms and legs wrapped around him. Even though I was hiding, I could see that her boobs (which are big enough for me to see from behind Dr. Blackwell's magnolia tree) were pressed against his back while he gave her a piggyback ride. My heart was racing.

All I can say is, thank you, Dr. Blackwell, for having a yard full of trees. I would have died if they'd seen me see them.

The one good thing about seeing them was

that it made me stop wondering how I feel about Matt. It doesn't matter how I feel about him, because seeing him with Jillian on his back made it clear how he feels about me.

He doesn't.

But it did make me wonder a whole lot of other things, and most of those things are about Billy. Did he kiss me because he likes me as more than just a friend? And if he did feel that way, does he still? Or is he mad at me because he thinks he can't trust me and now he feels that way about Brynn? And why do I suddenly feel like I like Billy as more than just a friend after seeing Matt with Jillian? Is it because I really like him or because I know Matt doesn't like me or because I'm worried that Brynn and Billy will be more than friends and I don't know where that leaves me?

I have so many questions. What I need are answers. I just don't know where to find them.

5:34 P.M.

May and June just asked me if I'd play Go Fish with them, but Mom said I couldn't play with them because Dad needs my help at the diner. She said one of Dad's waitresses went home sick and he needs me to pitch in. It beats sitting around and thinking about all my unanswered questions while playing Go Fish.

9:32 P.M.
Just back from The Love Doctor Diner
Found some answers

Waiting on tables all night was exhausting, but worth it because of what happened after I was done. When I was wiping up the counter, Dad said I looked really happy when we came home from the trip, but that I didn't look quite as happy now. He asked me if there was anything I wanted to talk about. There were lots of things I wanted to talk about—I just wasn't sure I wanted to talk about any of them with Dad.

But Dad brought two different key lime pies he had made over to the counter and asked me if I would do a taste test with him to pick which recipe I liked better. So we sat down together, and he cut into the first pie and put a slice on a plate. Dad handed me a fork and told me to dig in.

I told Dad it was a little tart. Then, I don't know why—maybe it was the tartness or the memory I had of eating key lime pie on our trip—but something made me just start crying. For a second I tried to catch the tears, but Dad saw.

"You sure there's nothing you want to talk about?" he asked. He looked at me like everything would be OK. It reminded me of the way he used to look at me when I was little and I'd fall or hurt myself. I probably should've been annoyed that he was looking at me like that, but I was more relieved than annoyed, and everything just started pouring out.

I told Dad what happened with Billy, and how I told Brynn about what happened, and what she said. I even told him what happened with Matt and what Brynn had to say about that.

"Now my friends are coming home from camp on Saturday and I have no idea what it will be like when they get here," I said. I told Dad that I can't help but worry that I'm not going to like how things end up.

I never thought I could have told Dad this kind of stuff. But he was pretty cool about it. He just listened while I talked. When I was done, he was quiet for a few seconds, like he was thinking about what to say to me.

"Relationships can be complicated," Dad said. He talked for a long time about boys and feelings and relationships. Some of it was embarrassing, coming from my dad. I laughed and told him that. But he reminded me that he used to write a column about relationships and that he wasn't called the Love Doctor for nothing.

Then he said two things he wanted me to remember.

"April, listen to your heart. If you really listen, it will tell you what to do."

When he said that, I knew immediately what my heart was telling me.

It was telling me that I like Billy, not just as a best friend, and that I need to talk to him and clear the air between us and tell him how I feel. It was exciting when Matt kissed me . . . but it felt right when Billy kissed me.

I told Dad that I hoped Billy being at camp with Brynn hasn't ruined everything.

That's when Dad told me the second thing

he wanted me to remember. He said not to assume the worst as far as my friends are concerned.

He talked about how it is human nature to believe the worst is going to happen, but it doesn't usually come to pass. "Trust your friends," he said. "Sometimes people surprise you, and I think your friends will surprise you in a good way."

I told Dad I hoped so, but I wasn't sure.

Then Dad said the thing to do was to stop thinking so much and eat some pie.

He cut a slice from the second pie and brought out two forks. We both took a bite. It was delicious—the perfect blend of smooth and sweet and tart. I'm sure I sounded like Goldilocks, but I told Dad this pie tasted just right.

After we had cleaned the plate with our forks, I thanked Dad for the pie and the talk and told him it had helped.

He gave me a big hug and said, "Anything for my number one daughter."

I smiled. Dad knows I like that he calls me that sometimes, because it could mean I'm his oldest, but it could also mean I'm his favorite.

He hasn't said it for a while, and to be honest, it was nice to hear it again.

Some day you will be old enough to start reading fairy tales again.

—*C.S. Lewis*

Saturday, July 13, 7:45 A.M.
Tossing and turning since 5:32 A.M.

I couldn't sleep last night.

My brain is racing. Today's the day Brynn and Billy come home from camp. I have so many questions I need answered, and even though I felt better after I talked to Dad, now I'm worried again. Dad told me I should believe in my friends and not expect the worst, but my brain doesn't seem to be able to follow his advice.

What if Brynn told Billy about Matt?

What if Brynn and Billy are a couple?

What if Billy doesn't feel the same way about me that I feel about him?

Billy and Brynn's bus doesn't get here until noon. Waiting won't be easy.

9:14 A.M.

I'm waiting. Not easy.

10:33 A.M.

I'm still waiting. Still not easy.

11:07 A.M.

I'm still waiting, and I just ate an entire shoebox of Captain Crunch. May just said I look like there's a baby in my belly, and now June keeps repeating it. Ugh, I'm having a food baby! NOT how I want to look today!

11:31 A.M.

The bus arrives in 29 minutes, and I'm going to be there when it does. I'm going to brush my hair, put on lip gloss, and find a tunic top to wear so when my friends get off the bus, no one will see my food baby.

11:32 A.M.

I can't find a tunic top.

11:34 A.M.

What am I thinking?!

I can't be there when the bus arrives. I have to talk to Brynn before I talk to Billy. I need to know what she's told him before I talk to him. I'm going to have to wait for them to call me.

I'm sure they will call the minute they get home.

Right?

12:09 P.M.

Brynn lives two minutes from where the bus stops. If it took her two minutes to get off the bus and two minutes to get home, she has been home for five minutes already.

She should have called by now.

12:17 P.M.

Brynn still hasn't called. If she doesn't call by 12:22, I'm calling her.

12:25 P.M.

I'm calling Brynn.

Still 12:25 P.M.

I just called Brynn. She said she was just about to call me, but before she could say another word, I told her I was coming over and I hung up. Was she going to call to tell me something good or something I don't want to hear? My stomach is a ball of fear, nervousness, and too much Captain Crunch.

2:10 P.M.
Just home from Brynn's

GOOD NEWS! Brynn didn't tell Billy anything about Matt. When I asked her about it, she said she couldn't even believe I would ask her that because she would never do that. "April, we're best friends, like sisters," she said. "And I would never tell anybody anything that you asked me not to tell. Not even Billy." Then I knew that there was nothing going on between Brynn and Billy. I could tell they were just friends like they've always been.

I wanted to give Brynn the biggest hug ever, but she wasn't done talking.

Brynn said she had two things to tell me.

The first was that camp wasn't the same without me. "It was fun," she said. "But I really missed you."

The second thing was that Billy missed me too. I tried to get her to tell me if she meant he missed me the same way Brynn did or a different way. I even showed her the T-shirt and picture frame I brought her back from Disney World and told her I wouldn't give them to her until she told me.

But Brynn did this zip-her-lip thing and told me Billy wanted to talk to me himself.

Then she said he was planning to come to my house this afternoon and that I better get home fast if I wanted to be there when he arrives.

I got home in record time.

5:15 P.M.
Billy just left
Best day ever!

I don't know where to start.

So much happened this afternoon when Billy came over. The first thing—after May and June jumped all over Billy and gave him huge hugs like he'd been missing at sea—was that right away, I noticed something was different. Billy grew while he was gone, and he was tan. On the cuteness scale, Billy went from a 7 to a 9.

The next thing that happened was that he gave me presents. Billy knows I love presents. And he had some really good ones. First he gave me a plaque with a photo he took of the sun setting over Silver Lake. It's so cool—I love it. He told me he made it for me in Arts and Crafts, and then he put it on my nightstand.

He started telling me all about camp, and even though it made me miss being there, it was fun hearing about it.

Then he gave me another present—a jar of lake water. He seriously brought me a jar of water from Silver Lake. We were sitting on the floor of my room, and he pulled this little jar out of one of his pockets and said since I couldn't make it to Silver Lake this summer, he brought the lake to me.

I opened the jar and it smelled disgusting, just like Silver Lake, but I loved it. I put the jar on my bookshelf. "That's the best present anyone has ever given me," I said. Then I told Billy that I had a present for him. I tried to give him the snow globe I brought him back from Disney World, but Billy said I'd have to wait my turn, that he still had more presents for me.

Billy took a piece of foil out of his pocket and opened it up. Inside was a s'more.

"It's from Final Campfire," he said.

I looked down at it. The marshmallow was just the right shade of brown. "It's perfect," I said.

He smiled at me. "You know what Camp Director Dan always says."

"If you don't want something to go up in smoke, don't hold it too close to a flame."

We laughed as we said the words together that we've been listening to Dan say at campfires for as long as we've been going to Camp Silver Shores.

I felt a lump in my throat as I looked at the s'more Billy gave me. He knows how much I love them. And Final Campfire is one of my favorite Silver Shores traditions. The last night of camp, anyone who wants to say something goes up to the campfire, puts a log on the fire, and says what they want to say to someone or to everybody. When everyone is done talking, the whole camp eats s'mores together, and then we do the Hokey Pokey. It sounds silly, but everyone ends up crying during Campfire and then laughing like crazy when we do the Hokey Pokey.

"I love it," I told Billy. "It makes me feel like I'm there."

"Pretend like you are," said Billy. "I have something I want to tell you. If you'd been at camp this summer, I wouldn't have said it to you at Final Campfire, but afterward, because I wouldn't have wanted anyone else to hear it." I looked down at the carpet.

Billy paused like he really wanted to make sure it came out right.

(I'm going to write out what he said as well as I can remember it, because it was amazing and I never want to forget it.)

"I know things were weird between us before camp. You've been my best friend for so long, and then . . . things were different. I was really confused before I left, but I had a lot of time over the summer to think. I wanted to write and tell you what I was thinking. I started a bunch of letters, but they never sounded right so I decided to wait until I got home."

Billy's voice got softer. "April, I missed you this summer."

When Billy said he missed me, I could feel my heart thumping inside my chest. It was so sweet the way he said it.

He kept talking, quietly, like he only wanted me to hear what he was about to say, even though we were the only ones in the room. "April, it sounds weird to say this, but . . . will you be my girlfriend? I really hope you will be."

Part of me wanted to laugh. The way Billy asked me to be his girlfriend sounded so old-fashioned and funny. But it was so Billy-like to ask in such a sweet, sincere way.

My talk with Dad at the diner floated through my brain. Listen to your heart, April.

I knew what my heart was telling me. Finally, I had an answer instead of just questions. "Yes, Billy. I would love to be your girlfriend."

Billy grabbed my hands, pulled me up off my bedroom floor, and started doing the Hokey Pokey with me.

You put your whole self in,
You put your whole self out,
You put your whole self in
And you shake it all about.
You do the Hokey Pokey
And you turn yourself around,
That's what it's all about.

When we were done, we were both cracking up, just like we always do at camp when we do the Hokey Pokey. Except that doing the Hokey-Pokey in my bedroom seemed even funnier. We couldn't stop laughing. Just looking at each other made us laugh even harder. Tears were rolling down my face.

We were laughing so hard that Mom came in my room to make sure we were OK.

I told her we were. We were more than OK. We were April and Billy, just like we've always been, only better.

The more things change,

the more they stay the same.

—*Alphonse Karr*

Today was Brynn's thirteenth birthday, which she celebrated at the Love Doctor Diner. I still can't believe that's where she ended up celebrating her birthday. It worked out in a funny way.

It started this morning when I called Brynn to wish her happy birthday. She was telling me that her mom said she can have a party when school starts, because it was hard to plan something for her while she was away at camp.

I said, "It's too bad we can't have a party for

you on your birthday."

June heard me say that, and of course she repeated what I said to Mom, who told Dad, who called Brynn's mom and said that it would be fun to celebrate Brynn's birthday at the diner. So that's what we did. Dad closed up early and we had a surprise celebration in honor of Brynn at the Love Doctor Diner.

Brynn and her mom and dad were there, and Billy and his family, and Mom and Dad and May and June and me. Dad served all of the Love Doctor Diner specialties: Fried chicken, potato salad, deviled eggs, biscuits, and shrimp and grits.

Mom made Brynn a "Birthday Girl" T-shirt and matching hat, which she insisted that Brynn put on.

I was a little embarrassed about the T-shirt and hat thing—though Mom has definitely made worse. But Brynn was a good sport. She even went along with things when May picked her up by the legs and said she was going to hold her in the air for thirteen minutes, one minute for every year of her life.

I guess the idea of it was really funny to May, who was laughing like a crazy person which made June do the same thing. It was mortifying, but also kind of funny, so I just shrugged my shoulders and made a kids-will-be-kids face.

I thought it was a cool way to handle things.

Mom seemed to think so too, because she put her arm around me and said something very parental about how I have shown a great deal of growth and maturity over the summer. Fortunately when she finished saying it, she told May to put Brynn down.

When dinner was over, Dad brought out a pie with candles in it and we all sang "Happy Birthday" to Brynn.

Brynn said celebrating her birthday with her friends and family at the Love Doctor Diner was great, and for the most part, I thought it was fun too. But it made me think a lot about the last time I was there with all of them, at the grand opening.

So many things have changed since that night.

At the grand opening, there wasn't one part of me that wanted to be at the diner. I didn't want to wear the jacket Mom made or serve pie to people I know or be any part of a crazy, themed restaurant smack in the middle of town. I didn't want anything to do with my family, and then Billy kissed me, and then Matt kissed me, and the next thing I knew I was stuck at home for the summer babysitting my sisters and going on a family vacation I didn't want to go on.

It's weird that my brain was so obsessed this summer with Billy and Brynn and Matt and what they were all thinking.

Now it all seems so silly. Things with Billy and Brynn are better than ever. Dad was right when he said I should trust my friends. Brynn is an amazing friend and Billy is an amazing boyfriend. In a month and a half I'm starting eighth grade, and Brynn says it is even more exciting to have a boyfriend in eighth grade than it is at camp. I guess we'll see (though I never did get to try it at camp). Even though a lot happened this summer, Billy, Brynn, and I are still the Three Musketeers, and hopefully, that's what we'll always be.

And then there's Matt. I spent so much time

worrying about what he thought of me. All I wanted to do was look and sound cool around him. But I have Billy, and it feels right. Tonight I was just happy to be at the diner with the people I love most.

Which I have to admit, besides my friends, is my family. Things with them definitely improved over the summer. I mean, they're as weird as ever. But I think maybe I'm different. I've been trying to be more patient, especially with May and June. Mom said one day they'll grow up and I won't recognize them. I asked her if that was a promise.

I think Mom and Dad have been trying too. They still say stuff that gets on my nerves, but I think they're starting to get the idea that I'm a teenager now.

And even though so much changed this summer, some things stayed the same.

As we were all leaving the diner tonight, Brynn stuck a pretend microphone in my face and said, "Tell us, April Sinclair, as an experienced thirteen year old, do you have any advice for the birthday girl?"

It was so Brynn-like. I had to think about my answer. I decided to keep it short and sweet. "If you don't want something to go up in smoke, don't hold it too close to a flame." I glanced over at Billy, and he winked at me.

I still can't believe my friends were at camp without me. One thing I can say for sure is that I never EVER want to miss camp again. But I can also say that even though the summer didn't turn out the way I planned, I think it worked out exactly the way it was supposed to.

Acknowledgments

This book was written with the help of so many people.

First and foremost, I'd like to thank my family. To my parents, Kenneth and Annette Baim, and my sisters, Leigh Mansberg and Karen Reagler: You have given me a lifetime of love, laughter, tears, and memories. For all of that and more, I am eternally grateful.

To my wonderful agent, Susan Cohen of the Gersh Agency: all my thanks for all you do (and you do a lot)!

To my amazing editor, Anna Cavallo, and the rest of the incredibly incredible team at Lerner: from start to finish, thank you for all you've done every step of the way.

To Gloria Rothstein, an amazing friend and a meticulously careful reader: thank you, thank you, thank you! (I can't thank you enough!)

To all the students at all the schools I have visited: Thanks for all your input over the years. I hope you've learned even a fraction as much from me as I've learned from you.

And of course, my deepest thanks to my children, Becca and Adam, and to Albert. I love you all with all my heart.

About the Author

Laurie Friedman can sympathize with April Sinclair. Ms. Friedman grew up in a small town in the South; she had two little sisters, a mom who made a lot of her clothes, and a dad who gave a lot of advice; and the summer she turned thirteen, she went on a family vacation while her best friends went away to camp. If you were to ask her parents, they would say that her attitude at thirteen was a lot like April's. If you were to ask Ms. Friedman, she would say that although she didn't want to go on the trip her family took that summer, it turned out to be a lot of fun.

Laurie Friedman has written more than thirty books for young readers. She is the author of the award-winning Mallory series as well as many picture books, including *I'm Not Afraid of This Haunted House*; *Love, Ruby Valentine*; *Thanksgiving Rules*; and *Back-to-School Rules*. She lives in Miami with her family. You can find Laurie B. Friedman on Facebook or visit her on the web at www.lauriebfriedman.com.